Murder Inc.

RI

Outskirts Press, Inc.
Denver, Colorado

Murder, Inc.
All Rights Reserved
Copyright © 2006 Sherri Rabinowitz

Outskirts Press
http://www.outskirtspress.com

ISBN-10: 1-59800-282-1
ISBN-13: 978-1-59800-282-9

Printed in the United States of America

Acknowledgements

I would like to thank Web Warrior and Bard Eyes for helping me to make my dream come true.

Michele for the hard work on this book which was just what I had imagined. Day for helping with editing and making my story into a novel. Lynka, Carol, Larisa for encouraging me when I kept running into road blocks and giving me the courage to keep trying.

I would also like to extend a deep loving thanks to my family for their unswerving support and love for all my adventures. For parents who said I can do anything I set my mind to and a brother who simply said, "Go for it!"

Thank you all, If it wasn't for you my book would not exist.

Ri

About the Author

Ri lives in sunny Southern California where she had spent most of her life. She was born in Garden Grove just a stones throw from Disneyland, which explains her weird imagination. At six months she started her adventure of moving all over the place. Starting in several locations in Los Angeles County then to Toledo, Ohio and Sumerset, New Jersey. She returned as a pre teen to the different locations in the San Fernando Valley a suburb of Los Angeles.

Ri has been writing she was a small child. She was inspired by Ray Bradbury and Agatha Christie. She loved writing but has had to make a living in a varied number of ways. She worked as an actress, a travel agent and in several forms of customer service. Her passion though has always been writing. She loves and enjoys both reading and writing fan fiction. Murder Inc is her first attempt at original fiction.

Enjoy.

Summary

Alex Bennett led a double life. She was known the world over as the highly successful founder of a toy software company. But she was also the head of the infamous Murder, Inc. A situation she didn't want but felt an obligation to fulfill until she met the lovely Patty Darcy and suddenly she wanted to just be the head of Toy Software. Now she had something to fight for. Will the love of the sweet woman help her get out from under the weight of family obligations? Will she be able to share a life with this good woman?

Chapter One
The Meeting

Of all the things Alexandra hated and despised one of the worst things for her to do was shop. To make it even more horrid was that she hated crowds so Christmas shopping was at the top of her list. Add to that the rudeness that seemed to accompany the season and she was in a very grumpy mood as she entered the malls parking lot and selected a spot close to the entrance. Christmas was a peak time for her company, so she was very busy with work. She also had few friends and almost no family members with whom she shared the season; it held no special warmth or holiday spirit for her. Sitting in her brand new, red Lexus sports car, she stared at the double glass doors that were enclosing the cacophony of sights and sounds: jingling of bells, ho-ho-ho's, and the multitude of shoppers descending on the festively decorated stores like a horde of locusts. Still, there was no getting around the few gifts she did have to buy. Alex sighed deeply. *Might as well get it over with.* She exited her car, checked to see that it was secure, and in a determined stride, approached and entered the crowded mall.

Alex was the sort of woman that would ordinarily stand out

in a crowd, but the frenzied holiday shoppers took no notice, intent as they were on their single-minded pursuit of the perfect gifts. *Ah, one of the only benefits of the season,* she smiled to herself, basking in her anonymity. Assessing her surroundings to decide where she should embark on her own dreaded excursion through the decked halls, Alex spotted the little cafe outside of Macy's and decided to fortify herself with a cappuccino first.

At the stand, a cute strawberry blonde smiled at the attractive raven-haired woman as she approached. *Wow! What beautiful eyes,* the clerk thought to herself as pale blue eyes smiled warmly back at her.

Wow! What beautiful eyes, Alex's thoughts unconsciously echoed, as the vibrant green eyes shone at her with anticipation. "Hi. May I have a chocolate cappuccino, please?" she requested, tilting her head slightly to one side.

"Sure, coming right up." Patty was thinking that the tilt was endearing as she went about preparing the requested beverage. *She is a beautiful woman. I don't think I have ever seen anyone like her in my life.*

Alex was enjoying watching the girl work when a sudden movement to her right caught her eye. Without any prior hint of motion on the tall woman's part, she effortlessly vaulted over the counter and protectively shielded the girl with her own body.

Suddenly there was terror everywhere as shots rang out, and a patron that was only two feet from Alex lay dying in a spreading pool of his own blood. Alex looked over the counter directly into the eyes of the killer. Her eyes held no fear; instead they were scalding the gunman with anger. The assailant looked stunned, freezing for just a moment, then ran out of the mall looking over his shoulder--sure he was going to die.

Maybe later, Robby. I have more important things to look into right now.

Alex slowly lifted herself up off the small blonde. Patty

was not moving at all and after careful examination, Alex determined that she was in shock. Unfortunately Alex was well aware of the effects on the human systems, since she caused this condition more times than she wanted to think about. "Are you okay?" she asked quietly, gently touching the young girl's arm.

Two scared, unfocused green eyes looked right through the questioner. *Oh God,* thought Alex. Her heart lurched at the sight of the shaken woman. *Poor kid.*

Alex was frantically trying to get the young woman to focus on her and not on the activities around her. That she was now so focused on Patty came as a complete shock. Her instincts were screaming at her to get the hell out of there, but she could see the police at every exit. Besides, way too many people had seen her make the dive to save the young woman beside her. Since she had saved the girl, she would be damned if she was going to move an inch until the poor clerk was herself again.

"Hey, are you all right?" she repeated, taking each hand and turning the young girl so she faced Alex and not the chaos and confusion behind them. "Come on. Look at me, only at me. Follow my voice and focus on it 'til you come to my eyes, and then don't take your eyes away from mine."

Very slowly, frightened eyes met her own. *Come on,* thought Alex, *I need you to be all right so I can get the hell out of here. Damn that dumb rookie, We are going to have quite a chat when I get back.* Alex swallowed her anger; she couldn't allow her mind to think about herself, she had to focus on the girl and bringing her back to the present. She briskly rubbed the wrists she held. *Come on, please snap out of it. Look at me.*

Patty tried hard to form words, but she couldn't seem to get her brain to function.

"It's okay. You're all right. Everything is going to be okay," Alex said reassuringly. *God, I hope to hell that it is.* Instincts screaming at her to flee, she glanced assessingly at the gathering crowd once more. *I should get the hell out of here....*

3

But I can't. Look at her. She is in shock ...I can't desert her now...It's my fault.

"Ma'am?" said a young officer from behind Alex, breaking her away from her own disturbing thoughts. She looked at the officer with piercing blue eyes. Suddenly, getting out of there was an impossibility. She had to protect this innocent, that was her responsibility right now.

"Yes?"

"Um…I understand from a number of these folks that you actually saved this young woman's life. Did you see the assassin?"

Oh shit, Now I have to protect my rookie and this innocent, Come on, Alex you have been in tougher situations. Think, girl, think. The lie rose smoothly to her lips. "No, I was too busy protecting the young lady from flying bullets"

The young man nodded as he wrote her words into his notebook. "Understandable." Then he turned to Patty and asked , "Did you see him, Miss?"

"I…I…" Patty shook her head and burst into tears.

"Can't you see she's in shock? Let her get her senses back for God's sake. Where did you get your training? The Marquis De Sade…"

"Ma'am, I'm just trying to get the report completed…"

Alex caught her breath and began to breathe deeply to prevent herself from launching off into another tirade. *What's wrong with me? Calm down, old girl. All you have to do is be a polite and innocent witness,* she thought to herself as she brought her breathing under control and smiled sweetly, "I'm sorry, officer. I'm upset too, I guess"

"That's all right, ma'am. Perhaps we can get her statement after she has seen a doctor." He once again focused on the very upset young girl. "Miss, would you like an officer to take you home?"

Shit! She's in shock now, but what if she did see something? I need to convince her that she didn't get a clear view of the man. After all, she was pretty shook up and there were flying bullets and glass. What could she have seen clearly? Yeah, that's good…besides I can't let someone who is so shook up drive, especially when it was my employee that caused this…I need to take this innocent home, not let the cops do it. "That won't be necessary. I'll take her," Alex volunteered, surprised as the words fell out of her mouth. She took one look at the shaken young woman and was very glad she'd said it.

Patty suddenly was more aware of her surroundings, "Oh….I….drove here…I can…."

The officer shook his head, "No, Miss, The lady is right; you're all shook up. I think it would be best if you were taken home. You are both allowed to leave. I do need to have your names, though.

Patty nodded. Still crying, she whispered, " Patty Darcy."

The officer looked at Alex. She took a deep breath and said quietly, "Alex Bennett."

The officer looked stunned, "*The* Alex Bennett? The one who owns the Bennett building and Toys Inc.?"

Alex nodded her head briskly.

"Okay, you are both free to go. I know how to reach you."

*****

Alex made Patty as comfortable as she could in the passenger seat of her sports car. She carefully adjusted the seatbelt and closed the passenger door. Alex was very worried about the sweet, golden-haired woman. She hadn't uttered three whole sentences since the shooting, and she still had the look of someone in deep shock. Alex closed the door to the passenger's side and thought, *I have to calm her and then find out what she knows . Poor kid, she is really shaken up…not that I blame her: You're doing your job one minute, and the next you're lying on a floor strewn with glass with some strange woman on top of you. Not exactly an every day occurrence.*

"Miss Darcy, could you give me just a little hint where to go? Please?" Alex asked her companion with an understanding smile on her face.

Patty *didn't* look up. She was staring at her hands in her lap and muttered quietly, "Lime and Republic."

Alex nodded her head and started the car; at least she now had a direction to go. *I need to get her to tell me what she knows, and I also need to get her back on track. This is ridiculous; I'm in charge of two multi-million dollar operations and I can't figure a way to proceed with this simple inquiry...I know!*

"That was really scary. Did you see all that glass shatter?" *There*, thought Alex, *that ought to get her talking and keep me out of this, I hope.*

Patty shook her head, sobbing quietly, "No...I was facing the other way. I heard bangs...then a whirring noise by my ear. Then you jumped on top of me and then ...nothing..."

"Wait, back up....Did you say you heard a whirring noise by your ear?" Alex asked tensely. Her heart was thumping wildly. *One of the bullets almost took off her ear?* she thought to herself, thinking that it better not be that.

Patty nodded, "Uh huh....I ...don't remember much after that. I guess I fainted..."

"I don't blame you. Where do I turn?" she asked quietly. *I am going to kill Robby! He almost shot this bystander. If I hadn't been there...*

Thankfully, Patty interrupted her thoughts, "Oh, it's that apartment building right there."

Alex pulled up and parked the car in front of Patty's building. It was a pretty Victorian style house that had been subdivided into apartments in the 80's. Alex admired the structure and design of the old white building.

Getting out of the car, Alex assisted Patty as she exited. She was literally shaking all over. Alex briefly considered carrying the young woman to her apartment. It probably would have been more efficient, but she knew it would embarrass her companion. So, she gently guided Patty until she finally got the poor woman to the front door of her apartment.

Once inside, Alex's discerning eye took in the entire studio in one glance. She was very pleased with what she saw. It was done in college girl chic with a little country style thrown in, but it was done tastefully with a knowing hand. The girl had a natural flair. Alex smiled to herself, deeply pleased by this.

There was a large combination couch-trundle bed in cobalt blue against the back wall of the apartment, upon which Alex gently deposited the shaken woman. The kitchen area was to her right, separated cleverly by one of those dividers you buy at Aaron Brothers that provides frames for pictures in it. It was filled with family photos that Alex took a moment to admire. She then pulled a crocheted quilt from a large chair beside the couch and gently covered Patty with it. She noticed a bookshelf to her left gorged with paperbacks from top to bottom. Across the room was a huge floor-to-ceiling armoire that had a small television set, an older VCR and a boombox CD player all of which look like it was in second hand but good condition. She suspected that the tapes and CD's were hidden within the drawers of the beautiful old piece.

Suddenly a white ball of fluff landed in Patty's lap. It was white Persian kitten. There was the first sign of the girl Alex had originally noticed as a smile of greeting was reflected on Patty's pretty face. It made Alex smile too. Then, as the relief took hold, Patty bent her head and started to cry into her cat's soft fur while she hugged it close to her. "Oh, Maddy...Maddy," Patty mumbled as she continued to cry on the cat.

"Miss Darcy, would you like me to get you a glass of water?" Alex asked the girl compassionately, gently brushing a lock of hair behind her little ear.

Patty looked up. It was the first time Alex looked into the pretty green eyes since their initial contact. The eyes were red rimmed and watery, but they touched the compassion in her heart. She felt so sorry for everything this young woman was going through. Compassion was not something Alex usually indulged herself in. It was a luxury she could not afford. This time was different, She was partially to blame for this innocent bystander's well-being, and so she felt the new emotion stir her.

Patty smiled at her and said quietly, "Could you just sit with me and Maddy 'til I'm a little stronger, then I'll make something for both of us. Please?"

I should go. I mean, she didn't see anything and she's safe now. She's a lot calmer. I have no reason to stay... Alex glanced at the open face gazing hopefully at her. *But I think I should make certain that she didn't see anything. Yes, I need to be 100 percent sure that she doesn't suddenly remember something 2 hours from now. And if she does, I need to be here to gently change her mind.* Satisfied with her own logic, she smiled and nodded, "Okay, I'll stay. Why don't you and Maddy lie down so you'll be more comfortable."

She tucked Patty into the couch and looked around. She went to the bookshelf and checked out the titles. Beside it hung a large framed certificate from the local college for an Associate Arts Degree in Literature. Alex was surprised but pleased by this discovery. Then she started to look at the books that filled the case and her face reflected joy upon discovering what types of books the young woman read. She glanced back at the now dozing girl, *This is a smart girl*, thought Alex with a smirk. She had practically every classic ever written. The most read ones were on the top shelf, and they all reflected strong, intelligent female characters. She had books on history and anthropology, as well as good helping of mythologies. There were biographies on many world figures, again mostly strong women. *That sweet little face is deceiving. She has a sharp mind in that pretty head. Mmm...Good. She could be the one I have been looking for, I mean...I could really use...someone I can talk to...like ...a friend...damn.* Alex shook her head and looked at the bookshelf. *It would be nice to have someone in my life that I could talk to without worrying. This might be a good opportunity to explore that possibility. That would certainly be a welcome addition to my life.* Alex nodded again at her own thought process and smiled. She gently brushed a finger against the titles on the shelf, pulled out the copy of Jane Eyre and sat down in the comfortable chair by Patty's side. She reached out and gently stroked Patty's hair and said soothingly, "Its going to be okay. Everything is going to be okay."

*****

She sat across the table from the nervous young woman as they both sipped some water.   As Alex reached to get an ice cube, she was stopped in mid motion by a gasp from Patty.

"What's wrong?" Alex asked instantly alert.

"You have blood splattered on you, would you like to use my shower," she asked, then realizing how that sounded, she stuttered," I...mean...uh..."

"I know what you meant, Miss Darcy. No, I think I'll regretfully leave you and go home to take care of this." She put the glass down a little too hard and it cracked, startling both woman. "I'm so sorry...I..."

"That's okay, Miss Bennett, I know you're upset..."

They smiled at each other, Alex looked away quickly confused by the emotions that she was feeling.

*****

Two hours later, Alex entered her building and headed for her office. The Bennett building was the center of the biggest distributor of toy soft ware in the world. It was also a front. A very good front, and Alex was damned if she was going to let one rookie ruin her business.

Tommy had no doubt of his boss's mood as she strode into her office. There was no friendly greeting or inquiry of any kind, just a brisk order and the slamming of her office door.

Alex sat behind her desk and booted up her computer. She grimly thought of the meeting ahead of her. "Maybe I should retire and give this side of the business to someone else? I can't let it affect me this way if I'm to...If I'm to what? Enjoy this? I haven't had that rush in quite a while, it's purely business."

She grimaced. "I guess that makes it pretty clear why I don't want to be here anymore."

Her thoughts were interrupted by a discreet knock. "Come."

As Tommy quietly entered her office, she looked sheepishly at him, "Sorry, Tommy. You know that I'm not pissed at you, right?"

Tommy smiled. "Alex, your apartment and car have been scraped and the clothing replaced. Anything else?"

"Yes, an innocent was next to me at the time of the action. I want her place very, and I mean very, discreetly scraped. Her car too. She's not to know, Tommy. I mean not even an inkling. Here's her address. Don't leave a single trace, same with her car."

"Do you want me to take any precautions with her..."

"Fuck no!!!" Alex's eyes went from calm to angry in a flash, and Tommy blinked.

"I don't want anything, I mean anything at all, to happen to her. I want her to stay whole and healthy. If anything happens, I mean if one of you guys causes her to break a nail, I will personally see to that person's discipline. Do you get my drift here, Tommy?" The rest of this statement was said very coolly, but Tommy could see the deadly glint in her eyes.

"Yes, Ma'am. Not a hair out of place, I promise."

It was silent in the room again, and then Alex took a deep breath and sighed. She sat down again. She was unaware that she had even stood up. Every protective instinct was aroused by this stranger. *What's up with me?* she thought to herself.

"I trust your discretion, Tommy." she said, smiling at the quiet man before her.

"Thank you, Ma'am." Tommy smiled gently at his boss. He sensed her confusion and suspected the reasons for it. He had known Alex for a long time.

"Don't worry, Boss. The innocent will remain as you like all innocents to remain--untouched."

Alex smiled at her secretary and friend. "Good man." She leaned back in her chair and looked up at him with intense blue eyes. "Now, to the other matter. Did you send for him?"

"He'll be here soon, Alex."

She nodded and Tommy knew he was dismissed.

*****

Before Roberto ever reached the penthouse, he knew he was in big trouble. The company had few rules. One was that no innocent would suffer in order for a job to be completed. Rule two was that Alex would never be involved in any scenario. He had blown both of them. He blew one through miscalculation, and the other through bad luck. *How the hell did I know Alex would be at the mall? She hates shopping,* he thought glumly to himself. He knew her penalties were swift and sometimes deadly, so he was more then a little unnerved as he entered her outer chamber.

Tommy looked up and nodded grimly toward the door. "Go on in, Robby. She's waiting for you."

Slowly he entered her beautiful office. It was tasteful and stylish, pure Alex. Alexandra Bennett was the CEO and founder of 'Toys by Me.Com' and ran that highly successful company gently but firmly. She was also CEO of Murder, Inc., which she ran with an iron fist. And Robby knew he was about to run right into it.

"Sit," the beautiful executive ordered. As he walked quietly to his chair, she waited with a grim expression on her face. She shook her head, "Two rules, Robby. Two fuckin' rules. Is there any reason I shouldn't have you taken care of this minute?" she asked, gazing at him with those pale blue eyes that held no hope for his escape.

To his credit he gazed back, his eyes full of penitence and answered quietly, "No, Ma'am."

She nodded her head and then started to pace behind her desk--back and forth, like a lioness in a cage. "Why, Robby? Why a place full of innocents?"

"It was the only time he was clear, Ma'am."

"But he wasn't, was he? Do you realize I got his blood on my favorite trenchcoat? Do you understand that two innocents were at a table two feet away, and another was behind the counter only a foot away? If I hadn't been there, that girl would have been hit by your stray." Alex shuddered at the thought of how close Patty had come to being hit.

"In hindsight, yes, Ma'am; but at the time, no, I didn't see those problems. I just thought it was a good opportunity to fulfill the contract," he replied honestly. Roberto knew one never lied to this powerful woman. She could detect a lie a mile away, and the results of such an infraction were always deadly.

Alex sat down and drummed her fingers on the edge of her computer pad.

"I really don't want you to be taken out, Robby. But you hit a place that I was at...."

"But, it wasn't in the book, Ma'am..."

Her eyebrow arched at the interruption and Robby shuddered. "Yes, Robby I was going to say that. You know how I feel about rudeness, Roberto." She said his full name in such a tone to emphasize the point. "You are on very thin ice, Robby. Since I did not get detained, and you didn't really hit an innocent, I will let this pass. But," she said the word with such quiet force it stilled his blood, "you will not get a third chance. Do you get me, Robby?"

"Yes, Ma'am. Thank you, Ma'am."

"Go." Roberto practically tripped running out of her office. "I'm getting soft." Alex thought to herself as she started to go through her in box.

*****

The buzz on her desk jolted her out of her dreamy thoughts of a certain strawberry blonde. "Yes?" she said into the phone after jabbing her finger down on the reply button, highly annoyed.

"Miss Darcy on line 2," Tommy replied calmly.

"Thanks." She looked at the blinking light. *Do I actually have butterflies?* she thought to herself. Then she shook her head in an attempt to clear out the little dears and hit line 2. "Miss Darcy, how are you?" Alex's voice suddenly became warm, and she hardly recognized it herself.

"I'm fine. Thank you, Miss Bennett. I just wanted to make sure you were all right. I was really worried about you," Patty replied sweetly.

Alex smiled. Someone was worried about her. Now that was a switch. "I'm fine, Miss Darcy, are you okay?" That stray bullet had passed way too close to this special young woman for Alex's peace of mind.

"Yes, I'm really fine thank you, Miss Bennett."

This formality is getting on my nerves, thought Alex as she drummed her fingers on her desk. "Would it break any rules, Miss Darcy, if you called me Alex? This Miss Bennett stuff is really beginning to bug me."

Startled, the young woman began to apologize. Alex shook her head and laughed. "I'm not upset. How about if I call you Patty, and you call me Alex? Not one of my employees calls me Miss Bennett. Not even the parking attendant."

Patty smiled and it showed in her voice," I'd like that, Alex."

"I would too."

"Um….I just wondered if you would go with me to police headquarters when I make my statement….I'm a little…Uh…I mean, I've never done anything like this before and you seem so…" She trailed off, uncertain as to how to best express the sense of security she derived from Alex's presence.

Alex smiled at the phone. It was perfect. She could gently guide the young girl's testimony. "Sure, I'd be happy to, Patty. When will you be available to go?"

"Um….I….well anytime really, Alex." The other woman sighed at the other end of the phone.

"What do you mean? What's wrong?" The butterflies were now airplanes buzzing around her stomach.

"My boss let me go," she replied simply with a tiny little sniffle.

That little sniffle touched off Alex's guilt and sympathy. She was more affected than she wanted to be, but she couldn't seem to help herself. "What? Why?" *The bastard,* she thought, suddenly snapping in half a mechanical pen she had been playing with. She looked down, a little surprised at the pieces of the silver pen in her hand. She put it down on her desk as she listened to Patty.

"For leaving work with out permission, and leaving the booth unattended, and a mess…"

"That is ridiculous…that's callous, cruel, heartless…"

"Alex, I did leave without permission…"

"Patty, you were in shock. What good would you have been at the stand if you couldn't even hold yourself up?"

"Alex, why do you sound so angry? He isn't mad at you."

Alex sighed deeply, "I just hate injustice, Your ex-boss has no compassion. It really makes me boiling mad when someone treats another human being that way." *Especially when that human being did nothing wrong, and it was partially your fault,Alex Bennett,* she scolded herself; and then thought, *Maybe, I should have a chat with Patty. She needs to know that she is a good person and deserves better treatment than her boss gave her. I know--I'll take her to a nice lunch. That would be a comfortable and unassuming way to talk with her and still accomplish my own agenda.* "Um…We'll go to the police station now, and then…Patty, would you like to have lunch with me?" She couldn't believe how insecure she sounded, like

14

when she was kid, just after her Mom died. She didn't expect that from herself, but she was pleased by Patty's immediate response.

"Wow, yes I'd love to!" replied Patty, obviously delighted.

Alex smiled, She liked hearing the younger woman sound upbeat; it was much nicer than the depressed sigh at the beginning of the phone call. "I'll pick you up in about an hour. "How about 1 o'clock?"

"Thank you, that would be perfect," There was an adorable sounding laugh accompanying the acceptance, and Alex found herself smiling broadly in response to it.

"See you at 1, Patty."

"I really look forward to it, Alex."

"So do I. Bye."

"Bye, Alex,"

There was a quiet click, and Alex couldn't help the warmth she felt inside. There seemed to be an inexplicable connection to this young woman. It went beyond the necessity of suppressing any information that Patty might have about the gunman, beyond the fact that Patty had almost been injured, beyond the clerk losing her job—Alex felt herself actually care about how all of those things were affecting the young witness. *I don't know exactly what it is, but I'm going to try and stay around her until I find out.*

"Bizarre," she said out loud in her empty office.

*****

"Ma'am." Tommy caught Alex as she left her office.

"Yes," she replied impatiently, wanting to be with Patty as soon as possible.

"The innocent has been scraped and left untouched. Do you have anything else you need done concerning her?"

Alex smiled. "If there is anything else, I will take care of it myself. I'm meeting her for lunch. And, Tommy, I don't want any unpleasant interruptions."

Taken aback and yet not totally surprised, Tommy simply replied, "Yes, Ma'am."

"Good man." And she was gone.

"Well, well a taste for innocents, huh, Boss?" he asked quietly under his breath.

Chapter Two
The Friendship

Sam looked up at the intimidating woman and then down at his sweetfaced employee. He really wanted to scream and yell. He wanted to call her an ungrateful bitch, But the moment after Patty said she wanted her money, Alex had stepped closer to her. With one look into those icy blue eye, he knew he had better watch his step.

"Patty, why can't you wait..."

"No, she can't. She politely asked for what's owed her, and now you will politely write out her check," Alex interrupted him in a quiet voice full of deadly steel.

This was the first time Patty had been exposed to this side of Alex. Strangely enough, it didn't scare her at all. She felt it was somehow familiar, and she knew instinctively that Alex would never direct that persona against her. There was some innate sense that even though Alex might get angry with her, as long as she was honest, Alex would always be the considerate, kind woman who took her home after the shooting.

Sam quietly wrote out her check and held it out to Patty, but Alex intercepted it before Patty could even move a finger.

Alex grabbed the man's arm in a vise-like grip and asked quietly, "This is it? What about severance pay, sick days, vacation? She's worked here six months; she's entitled to more than a measly two hundred bucks!"

Patty quietly attempted to defuse the situation saying, "It's okay, Alex."

Alex turned to her new friend, and in entirely different tone of voice with eyes that were suddenly warm and sympathetic, she said, "Patty, this is not acceptable. It is, in fact, against the law. Isn't it?" She addressed the last remark to the man she once more held in the grip of her icy eyes.

Patty was stunned at how quickly the woman could switch like that. Sam quickly wrote out a second check for four hundred dollars, "Is this acceptable, Ma'am?" he asked.

Alex studied it and said, "Yes, it will do. Patty, do you have anything in a locker here, or anything you should turn in?"

"No, Alex, I already gave Sam my apron and hat."

"Good girl. Okay, say goodbye and let's git," Alex said sweetly, with a beautiful smile for her new friend.

Patty grinned brightly back at her and then turned to Sam to say a spoken goodbye.

Uh, oh I am in big, big trouble, Alex thought to herself as she led her friend out of the mall. *I have done things in the last 24 hours that I have never even thought about doing before. And I'm so damn happy about it!*

*****

Leaving the mall, they went to the police station. Alex was concerned about Patty as she'd been very quiet since they'd left the mall. She didn't want to upset the young woman before she talked to the police, so she just kept a discreet eye on her.

Alex strode up to the desk sergeant, flashed a devastating smile and asked in a polite voice, "Would it be possible to see the detective in charge of the case involving the shooting incident at the mall…"

"Someone told you to do something and you're actually doing it; I can't believe my eyes and ears," said an amused voice from behind them.

Patty looked up into sparkling brown eyes of a tall, handsome man in grey suit. He was smiling affectionately at Alex and gave Patty a polite nod.

Alex looked just as amused, replying, "I do that once in a while, just to throw people off a bit." There was a definite laugh in Alex's voice, and Patty discovered yet another side of her new friend. In the small amount of time she had known Alex, she had already seen four sides of this complicated woman.

"I just bet you do. Okay, Alex, are you going to introduce me to your friend, or do I have to introduce myself? " He smiled charmingly at Patty and threw a teasing glance at Alex. "You must forgive her lack of manners; she really does know how to be polite, but she forgets around old friends like me."

Alex realized she relished hearing Patty described as her friend and tried to stop herself from indulging in that feeling; it was not the time and the police station was definitely not the place. She rolled her eyes at Jarret and said, "Patty Darcy, This is an old, old, old friend of mine--Martin Jarret. He's a kindly old codger, isn't he?"

"Watch that old codger stuff, or I'll get someone younger to take your statement."

"Oh, Jarret, That's great! Patty here has never had to do anything like this, and I'd prefer having a sweet gentle soul like you to do it." Alex was more then pleased. Jarret was an old friend, and he knew her secret, He'd protect both her and Patty.

"Shhh, Alex, you'll ruin my reputation."

"What rep? Everyone knows you're an old softie," Alex replied with a huge grin.

"It takes one to know one…"

"Let's go to your office you lecherous old goat…"

"Okay, okay, you win, come on you two," he said, laughing as he ushered them down the hall to his office.

*****

Two people were pacing nervously in Alex's outer office when the phone rang. Abruptly their heads whipped around, listening to Tommy's every word.

"Toys Software. Oh God, Alex, where are you?" Tommy's expression changed rapidly to shock. "Uh, Alex, You had a meeting and...but they're…Okay, okay, fine, I'll relay the message. Bye, Alex." He looked at the two people in his office as he put the receiver down and cleared his throat nervously, "Alex will not be in for the rest of the day."

The two people stopped dead in their tracks and stared at Tommy for a full minute. "What!" Val exclaimed. " I was under direct orders from her, Tommy. She had us practically in quarantine until she was able to see us, and now she's canceling!"

"Hey, I'm just the messenger, Val. She said to reschedule for 7am on the dot tomorrow. She also said to stress the 'on the dot' part, as she would be busy for the rest of the day."

"My God, Tommy!" she screamed.

"Do not scream in this office, Val. We are three feet from the executive offices of Toys, and you know how Alex feels about..."

"Being professional at all times around Toys. I know, I know, it's her mantra. Tommy, not showing for a meeting requested at 11am for 3pm is not exactly professional behavior either..."

"Val, Are you going to tell Alexandra Bennett that she is being unprofessional?" Tommy asked her, stunned and amused at the same time.

Val stared at him and then turned toward Roberto who said quietly to the agitated woman, "I'm in six feet deep of trouble already, Val. That's why I'm here. I'm not going to say anything but 'yes, Ma'am' and 'no Ma'am.'"

Val growled, shook her head wildly and stormed out of the office.Roberto quietly followed.

Tommy stared out the window, "What's up with you, Alexandra?"

*****

Patty was lost in the depths of pale eyes as she listened to Alex talking about recent trip to Asia to negotiate a contract for her software. She ate absentmindedly and listened to each and every word as if they would explain the secret of life itself.

Alex was just as transfixed by the sea green eyes before her. It was beyond her reason or understanding, but she felt so comfortable with Patty. She felt like she had known the young woman forever. She found herself talking non-stop to the young beauty, hardly believing that the chatterbox she heard was herself, Alex Bennet. Normally she was a very quiet person, but her nerves pushed her to keep nattering away to keep this young woman near her. Finally she concluded her story and decided to put the focus on her companion for a while.

"Patty, what are your plans?"

Patty looked down and started to play with her salad. "I don't know. I guess that I need a little time to recover from all this and then start looking for a new job. Thanks to you, I have some money that will give me a little bit of cushion to tide me over."

Alex swallowed the tremendous lump of guilt in her throat. *What can I do to help? I have to at least make her feel better.* "Patty, let's do something fun to take your mind off your troubles, Want to go to the zoo?" She looked hopefully into the pretty green eyes. She wanted to spend so much more time with Patty, and inwardly she cringed at that desire. *Oh boy, Alex, you are in such trouble.*

"I'd love to, I haven't been to the zoo since my grandmother died...But, Alex, don't you have things to do at your office. I mean, I gathered from what the officer said that you're an important person..."

Alex smiled wickedly at her friend and took a big bite out of her hamburger. Patty laughed at this playful side of her new friend. Alex really loved to hear Patty laugh; it made her feel good somehow, "Don't worry about the office. I took the day off. Sometimes it's good to be the boss. Now, let's finish up so we can enjoy the zoo. We can have dinner at my place. Unless, of course, you have plans?" Alex asked, shy for one of the only times in her whole life.

Patty eyes sparkled at the prospect, "No, I don't have any plans. I'd love to have dinner with you."

*****

Alex drove Patty to her mansion and then escorted the young woman on a tour around her home. Instructing the butler that there would be two for dinner, she settled her new friend comfortably in the living room.

Alex then sitting down next to her on the beautiful, comfortable brown leather couch, smiled proudly and asked quietly, "What do you think?" She was amazed to find that she was nervous about Patty's reply. *What the hell is the matter with me?* she thought to herself.

"I think it's beautiful, Alex...Wow! You have incredible taste. I'm so in awe of you. You've accomplished so much. I'm amazed..."

"Whoa, slow down. First off, I inherited this place and the money to start Toys. The only thing I've accomplished is to make my idea a success, which made more money for my company and, I also redecorated this place. My mother had it in 1950's modern, you know the uncomfortable kind of modern? Yuck. I like this look with antiques and classics. Do you really like it?" Alex asked her new friend.

Patty smiled brightly, nodding her head, "Of course. It's beautiful. I love this stuff. I browse at the flea markets and the stores in the mall during lunchtime. I like to sometimes imagine I own stuff like this, Silly huh?"

"Why silly?"

"Alex, I couldn't even afford this small end table. I just like to admire it. I know I'll never own it," Patty replied sincerely. Alex had an overwhelming desire to invite her to stay forever. She knew that it was ridiculous, and she would have to get to know her better before she even entertained the idea of asking her. Her heart and instincts screamed that she could trust Patty, and that she was the one Alex had been waiting for, but she knew she had to be cautious.

"You never know, Patty. One day you could own your own company and then we could have matching estates," she finally replied with big smile.

Patty's eyes widened and she shook her head fiercely, ."
I'm not like you. I couldn't run a company. "

"Patty, I really believe that you think too little of yourself. I see so much potential in you. " Patty had lowered her head. Alex made the girl keep eye contact with her by taking a long elegant finger and gently bringing her chin up. Alex suddenly had to swallow as she looked into those beautiful green eyes and cleared her throat to continue. Her voice was quiet and soothing.

"You are extremely bright. I think I have more confidence in you than you do."

They stared deeply into each other's eyes for a long time until a discreet cough made them both jump. They hadn't heard the butler enter the room as they were both so intently staring into each others eyes, Their souls reaching out to each other.

"What is it, Henry?" Alex asked gruffly, annoyed at his interruption.

"Ma'am, dinner is served," Henry replied with studied dignity.

"Thank you, we'll be there in a minute."

Henry nodded and withdrew.

Alex explained her bit of terseness. "He was from my parents' time, and he can be very maddening."

"He was just doing his job, Alex," Patty replied gently. "You'd have been upset if we missed dinner, wouldn't you?"

Not really, thought Alex. She nodded and smiled saying, "You're right. Come on, let's eat."

*****

Alex sat at her beautiful redwood 19th century dressing table. She was brushing her long raven hair and staring into her own big blue eyes in the mirror. With great conviction, she said to herself out loud, "Alex, you are so much trouble. You're falling in love. Damn, and you don't even know if she is a member of your club. I will not do a damn thing about these feelings. I'll just let this go naturally. I will not do anything to lose her, or jeopardize this precious friendship, damn it."

She looked at her reflection and shook her head at the force of her own words. Then she started to gently smile as she thought about her dinner with the beautiful young woman. Her eyes widened in the mirror as she remembered the feelings of loss that knifed through her as Patty's car pulled out of her long driveway to the road beyond. What was really shocking to Alex was that she felt no panic at these new feelings. She was excited and very happy.

"Oh boy, I am in really big trouble here," she said out loud to her image as she continued to brush her hair, her face reflecting the joy she felt.

*****

Alex entered her office the next morning to handle her delayed meeting. She smiled at Tommy and said a quiet, "Good morning."

"Good morning, is it Ma'am or Alex?"

24

Alex laughed good-naturedly and replied, "Alex. Sorry Tommy. You didn't deserve that. I must say I am looking forward to seeing Val and Roberto this morning. It should be a lot of fun."

Tommy chuckled and shook his head, "You're something else, Boss. Are you going to...take care of..."

"No, Like I told you yesterday I realize some of it was because he was cut loose too soon. Some of it was pure accident. His punishment should be very interesting. I can't wait to tell him. Valerie will also be included since she is responsible for turning the poor guy loose far too soon." She walked to her office and then turned to face Tommy again. "I'll go get stuff sorted in my office. Book this for about an hour, and then I need some time with my directors from Toys. I have a bunch of new...."

"Boss, What about your meeting with Uncle Vito?"

"Oh crap, I forgot all about that. Call him and ask him if he can make it a bit later..."

"Reason?"

She raised an eyebrow and he laughed and said, "Enough said."

"Good man."

*****

"Tommy, Alex said 7am sharp. We are here at 7am sharp! What the hell is going on!! "Val yelled at the unfazed young man behind the desk.

Tommy looked up and calmly said, "She's busy. She'll call you when she's ready. Why don't you sit down? And stop yelling. You know she doesn't like that," said Tommy, who knew that this was part of their punishment. Alex was just working on her computer, catching up on some reports for her meeting with her directors for Toys. She had acquired a bunch of new software, and she was going to present the information to her staff. She was excited about all the new product, but she was enjoying making her MI people sweat a bit.

There was a buzz from Tommy's intercom, and he nodded toward the door. Two very nervous people entered Alex's office. Alex didn't look up; she just said in a deceptively calm voice, "Sit down." She finished off her report and checked her email while watching the two fidget out of the corner of her eye. *I am really enjoying this way too much. I love to see people from MI squirm. Damn it Dad, I hate, despise and loathe what this division does. Why did you stick me with this? Was it a punishment because I wasn't the perfect daughter you wanted? Why the hell didn't you give it to Unc and leave me my life?* she thought morosely to herself and sighed. Then she took a deep breath and made the necessary adjustment in her thoughts and facial expression before she finally looked up at the two squirming people in front of her, their discomfort causing her to smile slightly.

"Well you two made a mess of this didn't you?" she asked quietly. One lift of an eyebrow silenced Val's expected outburst. "Don't even start with me, Val. And sit all the way down because you damn well may fall down when you hear all I have to say. I have talked to Vito, and you are both off assignments. You, Val, will personally re-train our friend here all the way from the very beginning. Just like he was a fresh recruit…"

"But that's not fair…"

"It's better then dying, Val. That is what my Dad's punishment would have been for you if he was still sitting in this chair. Both of you! Not only Roberto for screwing up, but you too, Val. He would have taken you out for not training the kid right."

Silence descended over Alex's office like the final curtain in a play as the truth of what Alex had said sunk into their heads. Alex looked at Robby who was studying his hands in his lap. Then her eyes flicked to Val, whose tanned face was white as a sheet. "Good, now that you're both calm and quiet, I'll explain to you what will happen next. Tommy will give you your travel documents to the farm. I want you to turn in all of your equipment, I mean it Val, every single thing. I don't want you to bring a thing with you. You're both starting from scratch. Dismissed." She then calmly turned toward her computer and began to work again on her overwhelming email.

The two shocked people got up and quietly left her office.

She looked toward the now closed door and said quietly to herself, "Forgive me Dad, I can't and won't do it your way. Let the family be hanged."

*****

After her board of directors meeting with Toys Inc., Alex returned to her office in a very good mood. It had gone exceptionally well, and the staff was excited to sink their teeth into starting the new software line. She had a big smile on her face when she saw her assistant, "Hi, Tommy. That was a great meeting."

Seeing the good mood his boss was in, he was hesitant to announce her visitor. She loved her Uncle Vito, but he was here because of how she'd handled the mall incident, and she would not enjoy a confrontation with her only living relative, "That's great, boss," he replied with a smile. "Um... your Uncle Vito is waiting in your in office. He didn't look too happy, Alex."

Alex's wide smile quickly disappeared as she responded to her friend and assistant. "I didn't expect him to be happy about it, Tommy. But, If he wants me to continue in this position, he'd better accept what I decide to do; or I will shove this whole damn division in his lap. I'd happily move the whole operation to Las Vegas and let him run it..."

"Whoa...Boss what brought this on?"

"Exhaustion and pressure....my conscience..." She took a deep breath, "I 'd better get this over with," she said as she smiled sadly at Tommy and entered her office.

"Can't say I blame you, Boss," he muttered under his

breath.

Uncle Vito stood up as she entered her office and immediately started berating his powerful niece, "What the hell do you think you're doing, Alexa?"

"Sit" She replied sharply.

Vito was a small round man and under normal circumstances, his appearance would be described as kindly, but his face held a mask of confusion and anger. He was about to argue with the girl, but the look of carefully hidden rage on her face changed his mind quickly. He sat down and looked up expectantly into angry blue eyes.

Alex sat on the edge of her desk. She took a deep breath to calm herself and crossed her arms as she lifted an elegant eyebrow in a gesture well known to her only living relative. She was really trying to be patient with her uncle. He had been the only source of love in her life since her mother died when she was a little girl.

"I know you expect me to run this place the way Dad did, but I'm not him. I only do this because of a sense of obligation to him and to you. I love and respect you, and I care what you think but, damn it, I will not fry someone for an honest mistake! I will not lose two good people because of rules older than time itself. If you can't accept this, then I will be happy to transfer this whole division to your care. Frankly, I do not want the damn thing. I never did!"

Vito simply stared at his niece. He was unable to make his mouth work, and it took a full minute for him to respond. Of all the things he'd expected her to say, this was not it. "Alex…Why? I mean…why would you give it to me, honey? You know why your father gave you the leadership. You are so powerful and I…I…"

Alex's face softened, and her voice was sympathetic. "Unc, Dad was very harsh in his judgments. He always was. Even towards me, his only child. Do you remember what his reaction to my lifestyle was when I tried to tell him why I didn't want to marry who he had arranged for me?" she asked, an ironic smile contorting her pretty face.

Vito nodded, "Yes, pure rage. He did really love you; and since your mother died, you were all he had left. I guess that finally tempered his reaction, if not to acceptance, then at least to some form of tolerance. Honey, do you really want to quit?"

Alex nodded her head, "I have for a very long time. Unc, I met someone. It's changed everything." Alex's mind drifted as she thought of her pretty blonde friend and how she was slowly falling for her. Even though she wasn't certain how Patty felt, or if she even could feel the same way, she'd have to leave the dark world of Murder Inc. to ever have a chance at a normal life with her. Suddenly there was the clearing of a throat, and her head whipped around to meet her uncle's compassionate eyes. Her cheeks were hot, and she knew she was blushing. "Um...Sorry, I'm in really deep trouble, Uncle Vito." She had grabbed a paper clip and was twisting and untwisting it, her eyes focusing on the piece of metal in her hands, "Um, I think I'm falling in love. Head over heels in love with someone. I don't know how she feels toward me, but I must be suitable for her if she does return my feelings in the slightest. And I can't be with MI around my damn neck. I really want to protect her from it. I hate it, anyway; I always have. Can't you take MI? I mean all of it...I'll continue here at Toys Inc., and you'll make your usual profit from Toys. I need to get out, Unc...I want..." Tears were now falling from her lowered eyes, "I want a life!"

Vito got up and crossed to his niece to gather in her in his arms in a comforting embrace. He hugged and soothed her as he did when she was child. He kissed the crown of her head and, as he always did, he put her needs first as he spoke gently to her. "This is really different, isn't it, honey? I haven't seen you cry since you were 7 years old and lost your favorite fishing pole," he said with a sweet smile. She looked up and met his eyes with tiny smile of her own. She nodded her head in response and lay her head on her uncle's broad shoulder. "Alex, I think you're right. You do deserve a life. I wonder though, if I am the best choice for the job. I mean, you know what your father thought of me…?"

Alex looked up into her uncle's sincere warm brown eyes, wiping her own with the back of her hand. "I really don't give a crap what Pop thought, Unc. You are a good man, and you far more suited to that division then I ever was."

"That isn't true, sweetheart. You know that you are very good at it. I see that you never liked it now…But Alexa, Murder Inc. changing hands will not cleanse yours. Moving the division and switching it to my supervision will not protect you. You still have made enemies. How will you protect yourself and this lucky girl?" he asked gently.

Alex nodded and moved out of her uncle's embrace. She walked to her large window and looked out at the skyline as she replied. "I know that, Unc. But…it's a start. We'll do this gradually. First we'll have the lawyers draw up the papers, then we'll reassign the staff to you." She turned toward him with an ironic smile on her face as she said, "You already have two that will be coming down next week, Val and Robby. I needed to give Val time to close out some obligations before they go to the farm, or it would have been tomorrow. It's a great punishment. Val will teach him from scratch. Just keep them there, and I'll transfer the others…"

"What if they don't want to…"

"That's what contracts are for, Unc. They are obligated to Murder Inc., not to me. They have to do it. If the documentation says you are in charge, they have to accept it. No arguments, no demonstrations, and if they do try to do that then they'll get the severest of penalties. There is no reprieve."

Uncle Vito knew that meant death, He looked at her in shock.

Alex shrugged her shoulders and turned back to the window, "I didn't write it. Dad did. They knew their choices; they all signed it. Dad always explained it clearly before a recruit was signed, as did every officer of the company."

"What about the contracts here? After they all move, will they still report here for a local contract?"

"No, Unc, Once you take over, I don't want anything to do with it. Toys Inc. will be my sole responsibility, and MI will be yours. You can have all the profit from it. I make plenty here. I need to begin to make the life I want to lead if I expect to find any sort of redemption or happiness," said Alex quietly, looking out the window as if she was trying to see her future.

Chapter Three
The Job

Alex sat in front of the computer in her office staring unseeingly at the same sentence on a marketing and sales report. Her mind was far away from work at the moment. It was on yet another job interview her friend Patty was attending. It had been a week since the shooting, and the poor girl had been on at least two interviews a day without success. She just couldn't seem to catch a break. Alex got up and went to her kitchen to refill her coffee cup. She had gone to lunch with Patty every day, and the girl was becoming more and more down hearted. She wanted very badly to help her, but she didn't want to ruin their fragile new friendship by interfering too much.

Suddenly, in mid-movement she stopped and stared straight ahead. "I've got it! I'll set up a mock interview up with Sarah. Maybe we can figure out what she's doing wrong." She walked back to her desk and put her empty coffee cup down. Picking up the phone, she called Tommy, asking him to connect her with the head of Personnel. While she waited, she fidgeted with a paper clip and thought, *If I could just observe an interview situation, maybe I could help her. I just don't understand this. She is bright and capable, and she has a degree for God's sake. She has to be doing something during the interview process to take herself out of the running. She's so shy, it could be anything.*

Tommy broke into her thoughts. "Sarah, line one; and Patty's on line two, Alex."

"Put Patty through and have Sarah hold on for a minute," There was ring on her phone, and Alex pounced on it, "Hey, Patty, How did it go?" Her voice was gentle and full of support. She knew her young friend's heart was literally breaking with every interview.

There was a deep sigh, and then a quiet shaky voice replied, "Not good, Alex. I just wanted to call and cancel lunch today. I don't feel very well..."

"Oh no you don't. Tommy is going to come over and pick you up. We're going to have a mock interview, and then we'll discuss it over a nice relaxing lunch," replied Alex firmly.

"We are? Why?" asked Patty, concerned by the idea of Alex going through all that trouble.

"Because I want to observe you while you interview. There has to be a reason for all this. You're my friend, and I just can't stand to see you suffer any more," replied Alex, her heart speaking for the first time.

Patty was touched, but she was just as scared of disappointing Alex as she was interested in finding out how she was messing up all these interviews. "Alex, Thank you. I really appreciate it, but I truly don't feel well..."

"Patty, Tommy will be over in 20 minutes. No more arguments." Alex was determined to discover whatever it was that was causing her friend to lose every job opportunity.

Another sigh was heard on the phone, and then a barely audible, "Okay."

"Good girl. And dress like you would for an interview, too. I want the whole effect, okay?"

"Okay."

"Patty, it's for your own good."

"I know, Alex, but what's the use? I know you care because you're my friend, but I…"

"Well that is one reason; and the other is that I hate an unsolved mystery. Come on, relax. I promise it won't be bad. Sarah, who is the head of my Personnel Department, is going to do the interview, and I will observe you from the kitchen. You know--well out of your line of sight."

"Can't you do the interviewing?"

"Yes, but I want to watch you and see how you act. Besides I want her input; it's her job after all, and she might notice nuances that I don't. She's a very nice and gentle lady. Don't worry, just be ready when Tommy comes to get you. Bye, Patty."

Another deep sigh, "Bye." Then Patty hung up.

Alex stared at the phone for a minute and drummed her fingers. Then she poked the intercom, "Tommy, go pick up Patty and bring her here; and please try to cheer her up a little on the drive over here, Okay?"

"No problem, Boss. She's a nice girl. It would be my pleasure to help you guys out. I hate seeing her so down too, not to mention what it does to your mood."

Alex rolled her eyes. "Just do it, Tommy," she growled.

"You got it, Boss."

"Good man." Then Alex picked up the phone to speak to Sarah, "Are you still there, Sarah?"

"Yes, boss. I'm being constructive--I was cleaning out my email inbox while I was waiting for you."

"Hey, that's a good idea. Could you do mine too?"

"Ha, Ha, very funny, Alex. What can I do for my mighty leader?"

"A hell of a lot. Take out a note pad: this is what I want you to do…"

*****

34

There was a timid knock at Alex's door. With a lifted eyebrow, Alex shook her head and walked over to answer the door. She smiled at her friend, looked her over appraisingly, and said in soft sweet voice that seemed to come from her only when Patty was around, "The outfit is perfect. You look very professional. Come on in. The first thing you need to learn is to knock more aggressively. Don't worry, we'll get to that." Patty walked in, and her eyes timidly skimmed the office. She looked so nervous, it almost broke Alex's heart. "Come on, Patty, calm down. This really is just a role playing game. There is no pressure. I don't expect anything. I just want to help you. I need you to relax. The first lesson, I guess, will be that you need to realize that you are your own best asset. You're trying to sell all your good qualities during an interview, and since you have a lot of good qualities, it's going to be easy." she said with a smile and wink. "Any interviewer wants to see the real you. Come on, let's meet Sarah," she said with a smile as she took the little hand and led her over to the personnel director on her couch. "Sarah, this Patty. Patty, this is Sarah, Now sit down, and I'm going to go to the kitchen and let you two get on with the interview while I observe." Patty muttered that it was nice to meet Sarah and sat down on the chair next to the couch. Alex went to the kitchen and sat in the chair she'd put in there to be comfortable while she watched. "Ok, Sarah take over. Be gentle," she commanded, as she sat tensely in the chair to observe her new friend.

"I always am, Boss," replied Sarah with a smirk. She put her hand out and shook the young woman's hand. "Ok, Patty, I'm as gentle as a lamb, so don't worry. Your friend wouldn't put you in a bad situation; you know that, don't you?" Patty nodded and smiled at Alex. Alex returned the smile and nodded her head encouragingly. Sarah smiled and got down on her knees so she was eye level and said sweetly, "Ok, this is what we are going to do. I'm going to interview you like any other applicant, and Alex will watch carefully from the kitchen. Then we'll eat lunch, and we'll discuss strategies for you. Okay?"

Patty nodded again and stiffened up immediately. Alex cringed inwardly, *This is not a good start, my friend. Calm down. You know we're on your side,* she thought as she watched the terrified, shy woman being interviewed by her compassionate Human Resources person.

*****

The three of them were now eating lunch, and Alex had teased and joked with Patty 'til she had relaxed and was acting like herself. After they were done and waiting for Tommy to bring the surprise dessert that Alex had ordered, she turned to Patty and asked, "Okay, are you ready?"

Patty looked at the two older women and nodded, lowering her head. Long fingers gently pulled her chin up until she was looking into intense blue eyes, "I'm first. Look at me, Patty. That was a major problem during the interview. People are wary if you don't look them in the eye. Your answers were excellent, but your voice was so low that I could barely hear you. A prospective employer is not looking at the fact that you're shy, just that you're avoiding eye contact and they can't hear your answers to their questions. You trust us, and yet you are so shy it was making me want to jump in and tell you to just be yourself. You are an intelligent ,wonderful person ,but the person interviewing you would never have known it." She chucked the quivering chin and said, "Don't worry, we'll fix it. Sarah?"

"I was right next to you, Patty, and I had listen really hard to hear you. You did have really good, intelligent responses, but I would have worried about hiring you. If I didn't have some prior information from Alex, I would never have known what a capable woman you are, you hide it so damn well." Sarah stopped when she saw that tears were falling from the now lowered green eyes.

Alex dried the eyes and said gently, "Please stop this, Patty. This is for your own good. In fact, what happens in this room now will help you for every business situation. Now, you look excellent. Your manner is fine. You just need to work on two areas from what I saw. We need to hear you, and you need to look the interviewer in the eye. Sarah?"

"I really liked your answers, Patty. You're very creative, and once you were comfortable with me, you are a very good conversationalist. If you could just do that right away, I think you'd do great. Um, Alex, can I speak to you for minute?"

Surprised by the sudden request, her head jerked toward Sarah with an inquiring eyebrow, "Sure. Just relax, kiddo. Wait until you see the great dessert I sent Tommy for. It will make up for all this, I promise you." With a wink and light touch on Patty's shoulder, she followed Sarah to the kitchen and tilted her head in question.

"I know she is a friend of yours, but how would you feel about hiring her yourself? We have an opening in marketing for someone in customer service on the phone. She would be great, because she wouldn't be face to face with the person and she's very personable."

Suddenly Alex was excited. To have Patty here all day every day would be a dream come true. And since the suggestion was coming from Sarah, a professional in the area of hiring, instead of herself, it would give Patty a lot of needed confidence. She tried to sound very calm as she answered, though her heart was going a mile a minute. "I think that's an excellent idea. You ask her, okay? It is your idea, and I want her to know she earned this by her answers not because she is my friend."

"No problem. As a matter of fact, she is getting the offer because of her answers. I wouldn't hire someone just because she was your friend, and you damn well know it."

Alex laughed and nodded. "I know that, just make sure she does. Go on and tell her while I get our dessert." Alex watched as Sarah went to her friend, her heart pounding with excitement at the prospect of Patty working for Toys. She went out to help Tommy with the huge banana splits, and she was beaming so widely that Tommy wondered what had happened in the office during the mock interview to make his usually taciturn boss glow with happiness. They carried in the desserts, and Alex had to keep herself from dancing around the room at the overjoyed expression on her friend's face.

"Did you know about this job, Alex?"

"Nope, I leave all that stuff to Sarah. So, are you the newest member of my staff?" *Please, please, please, say yes!!!* she thought to herself, mentally crossing her fingers.

Tommy watched the expression and the barely hidden hope and glee in his boss's bright blue eyes. He shook his head as he went to the kitchen to get them some napkins. *You are so hooked, boss,* he thought to himself as brought them both napkins and a pitcher of water.

"I don't know about Alex, but I think you're perfect for it. It popped right into my head as I was talking to you," Sarah said honestly to the flustered young woman.

"I've told you many times I think you're a bright and capable woman. If Sarah thinks you're the right person for the job, that's good enough for me. So?" she asked the blonde anxiously.

Patty looked into Alex's blue eyes and nodded, saying, "I'd like to."

"You're hired," Alex said with a smirk, "Set it up, Sarah. Now come on, let's eat. Look what we brought you, Patty," Alex said pointing to the banana splits with a huge smile.

Patty's bright smile got even bigger when she was able to pull her eyes away from Alex's and said with joy, "Oh wow! I love those. Thank you, Alex, you're the best," she said as she hugged the older woman to her. Alex was caught completely off guard, but she relished the contact and returned the hug with as much affection as she safely could. "You're very welcome, my friend. You're very welcome."

*****

The next morning Patty was pacing outside her apartment at 6:51a.m. She was so nervous that she was polishing off all of the dirt on the sidewalk by her constant pacing. Alex told her that a blouse and a skirt would be fine for her new job, so she had on her best, plus an old cashmere sweater that she'd kept like new. It had been a gift from her grandmother, and she kept it perfect in loving memory of her kindness. She was trying to relax, but she couldn't seem to calm her wildly beating heart. It wasn't just the great new job that she was nervous about, though that was compounding it. As the week had worn on, she'd found herself having strong feelings for Alex. She liked her from the very beginning. How could she not like someone so kind and patient with her? No one had cared about her like Alex since her grandmother died. She knew that the circumstances of their meeting had something to do with it. She knew that, for some reason, Alex felt almost guilty about the shooting. Though for the life of her, she couldn't figure out why. *I really like her...a lot. But, it's more than just like. The feeling that I get with her is the same feeling that I have gotten from some men. It's different though, too--I like it with her. I'm ...well, attracted to her. That is so weird. I never have been attracted to a woman before. I mean, I never even noticed women's bodies at the gym. I never look at them,* she thought to herself as she continued to pace. She suddenly stopped and stared out toward the horizon, *Okay, now this is really weird! I am more than attracted to Alex; I really love being with her. I feel special with her. What in the hell is wrong with me? Alex has just been kind to me. I'll screw this up just like I do everything in my life.* Tears stung her eyes, and she blinked furiously. She didn't want her friend to know she was crying, because then she would have to explain why. Until she'd met Alex, she'd thought she was just not interested in sex. Now she realized that she was attracted to a woman, and that this might scare her new friend away. *I'd better not say anything. I'll just keep it to myself. She is the dearest person in the world; I will not lose her.*

Alex was excited and very nervous as her limo pulled up in front of Patty's place. The strawberry blonde looked adorable in her shop girl skirt and little cotton top. The antique sweater set the look to perfection. If only her little friend didn't have such a serious face, she would look just the way she wanted her to. *Well, it's probably just nerves. I'll cheer her up,* thought Alex as she smiled at Patty and winked.

Patty bent down and smiled a little, Just seeing Alex already made her feel better. Alex had to take a few deep breaths because her friend was unknowingly giving her an eyeful of cleavage. *Breathe, damn you, breathe! Calm down. She has no idea she is turning you on, so stop it!* she scolded herself, using her iron control to calm her arousal. Alex beamed at Patty as she remarked, "Good girl, you're right on time.

Patty sat down next to Alex and closed the door. She looked a bit sheepish as she admitted, "Actually, I've been here for ten minutes."

Alex eyebrows shot up and her smile broadened. "Why so early?"

"I was nervous, and I couldn't stand the four walls around me," admitted Patty, looking down at her own hands as she mumbled, "I don't want to disappoint you and…"

Alex gently placed her hand on the girls trembling hands, "Patty, you couldn't disappoint me. I don't have any doubts about you. I would have offered you a job myself, but I didn't think you would accept. You don't know how grateful I was to Sarah, When she saw all the potential I see in you, I knew I wasn't blinded by….um, friendship." *Shit I almost blew that. I almost admitted my feelings. Watch it, old girl,* thought Alex while enjoying the tingle zinging through her body at the contact of their hands. She was glad that both the words and her touch seemed to calm Patty down. She looked comforted. For that, Alex was very grateful.

Enjoying the slight contact, Alex thought, *This is nice. Could I just accept this? Just friendship? Yes, I would be happy with this. It's enough to have Patty in my life. As long as I never lose her friendship, I would be happy.* She smiled at Patty and Patty smiled back, thinking much the same thing as the beautiful older woman.

This is good. I love being with her I won't blow this, thought Patty as the car sped through the city streets, taking the two confused women to Toys, Inc.

Chapter Four
Something More

"Good, Patty, perfect!" Alex was standing behind her with a hand on her shoulder. She gently squeezed in excitement. "I told you that you'd be good at this."

Patty was beaming as she put her hand on top of Alex's. "Thank you." There were tears falling down her cheeks. Alex gently plucked a tear and asked, "Why are you crying? What's wrong?"

"It's gratitude. Thank you, Alex. I…"

Alex turned her chair around until their faces were inches apart, "You don't need to thank me. Your doing this all by yourself. I'm just guiding you." She had her hands on both of Patty's cheeks, and she was staring into beautiful green eyes, and she just couldn't help herself. Slowly she lowered her head, and without even realizing it, she was kissing the woman of her dreams. Alex, now beyond control, deepened the kiss and sank into the softness of the woman she hadn't gotten out of her mind since she first laid eyes on her.

They parted and their eyes met, shocked by what had just happened. "Oh, my God, Patty…I didn't…I wouldn't…I'm so dreadfully sorry…" Alex felt tears sting her eyes as she stared at her own thighs, the desk, anywhere but at Patty. *Shit for over a week I have promised myself I would not do this. And then with a will of Jell-O, I break my own promise to myself and I do it…Shit!* she berated herself within her own mind.

Patty, on the other hand, was uncharacteristically calm, All the thoughts and feelings she had toward the older woman seemed to fall into place. *I love her.* She thought calmly to herself as she gently lifted the beautiful woman's head so she could look into those sky blue eyes she loved so dearly. Every time she'd looked at Alex, her stomach had tightened, and she'd felt a wave of emotions she couldn't quite identify before. Now that she knew what it was, she felt really contented for the first time in a long time.

"Alex, do you like me? I mean, did you kiss me because you felt some emotion in the pit of your stomach that you just couldn't resist? That's why I kissed you back." Alex's beautiful blue eyes widened in shock. "If that is the reason you kissed me, then there is no need to apologize. Ever since I first saw you, I felt something I have never felt before. For a long time I thought it was gratitude, but stronger; now I know it was love. Do you love me? Do you feel a connection?" Patty quietly asked. She was internally shocked at how sure she was of the answer that would be coming. It was as if she had been waiting for this moment from the second they met.

Alex had to clear her throat. She had so many thoughts and feelings tumbling together that she had to sort them out before she spoke so she would make sense. "I kissed you because I felt an overwhelming need to do it. Actually, I felt something from the second our eyes first met, but…I…well, I didn't want to scare you. I had promised myself I'd let you make the first move, that I would follow your lead, that I would not do what I just did." She looked into darkening green eyes in wonder and realized that her feelings were returned in full.

"Patty, I think we should take a really long lunch break," she said with a big bright smile, extending her elbow toward the other woman. Patty stood up and accepted the arm, smiling back just as happily. They walked out arm in arm together, to discuss over lunch the future neither thought existed until this moment.

*****

After a very stimulating lunch at home, which consisted more of necking than food, Patty and Alex returned to the office. Alex dropped Patty off with Peter--the head of her marketing department--for more sales training on the phone. Peter was also taken aside by Alex and given very specific instruction on whom Patty should and should not meet. Happy for the first time in her life, Alex was going to protect this precious woman from any contact with the darkness that was Murder Inc.

Part of that dark life was waiting in her office when she returned from lunch, She smiled broadly at Tommy as she strode into her chambers. "Are our two lost sheep in there, Tommy?"

Tommy smirked back and nodded.

"Good," she said with a wink as she turned to face an enraged Val and a quiet Roberto. "Well, children are you ready for your little trip? Did you enjoy the debriefing?" she asked as strode to her desk.

Val was hopping mad, "Oh, man, are you vindictive. A whole week of being told I stink…"

"I don't believe anyone used that phrase. They said you were clumsy and overconfident. You are good employee, Val. I would never allow anyone to say you stink. Now sit down," Alex said, calmly interrupting the tirade. She knew the debriefing session was tough and embarrassing; they were meant to be. The last week was to make sure they understood what they were facing now that they were heading out to the farm tonight, and then they were Vito's problem.

Val sat with a thud and looked at a quiet Roberto. "Are you

ever going to say anything?'

"Nope," Roberto said wisely.

Alex smiled. "Smart man." He met her eyes and saw the approval and was a bit relieved. "Now, are you all packed and ready for your little trip. Uncle Vito is all ready for you."

"You know, Alex, you're enjoying this way too much," Val glowered, her arms crossed.

Alex shrugged. "It's good to be the boss."

Val rolled her eyes, and Robby covered his mouth to hide the broad grin. The last debriefing session for the two of them was off to a flying start.

*****

Peter was standing behind Patty feeling very happy about his pupil's progress. *What a winner,* he thought to himself as he watched the young lady perform each new task just as he'd taught her. *Alex sure can pick them.* A smile reflected the thought as he glanced up to see Alex walking into his office. Peter smiled at his boss and nodded his head, adding a joyful wink. Alex smiled back brightly in pure reaction to her beloved's progress.

Patty looked up into that radiant smile and was dazzled by it. She blushed a deep red and asked quietly, "Why are you smiling like that, Alex?"

"Because from Peter's expression, I see you're doing as well as Sarah thought you would and I knew you could."

Patty looked up at Peter surprised. Peter laughed and patted her shoulder gently. "You are doing exceedingly well, my young friend. Sarah was right, Alex."

"Yep," Alex said laughing at the beautiful blush that was now covering Patty's entire face. *Damn, she is just too cute when she blushes like that,* thought Alex, extending her hand. "Ok, young lady, it's time for all little worker bees to go home."

Patty looked at her watch and was astonished it was so late.

"Wow, it's 5:15. I can't believe it; time went so fast! Um...Alex, could you drop me off at my place? I mean, I'm sure you have a lot to do..."

"Actually, I have other plans. Come on." She wiggled her fingers and lifted an eyebrow. Patty got up and went to Alex, placing her hand in Alex's elegant one. Once she was firmly in Alex's grasp, she was towed gently out of the office by the older woman. "See you, Peter," was heard from Alex, and a confused, "Night," was heard from Patty as they disappeared around the corner.

*****

Alex pulled her car into the parking lot of Bacal's, an exclusive clothing store. Leading a very nervous Patty by the hand, they entered the elite establishment. The décor and feel of the place suddenly terrified Patty. The trim was all done in gold leaf, and she was sure if she even accidentally brushed her hand against any of the furnishings that they would break.

Sensing Patty's anxiety Alex whispered reassuringly, "Relax, it's just a store."

"It's an expensive store. Alex. I've never set foot in place like this before."

"Well, this will not be a big deal after you get used to it. There is a first time for everything, and this is only the first of many, many visits. Relax, Patty, you're going to love it," she said softly, caressing her cheek and winking at her with a huge lopsided grin. Patty relaxed a little under Alex's tender loving care, but she still felt like a fish out of water.

A tall, elegant woman entered, haughtily sizing up the two women and deciding they were merely business class. "Yes, may I help you ladies?"

Alex groaned inwardly, She despised snobs of any kind, and this woman was a typical saleswoman-snob, judging people solely on appearance. "I'm here to see Katherine, please," she said politely.

"Do you have an appointment?"

"No. But if you would just tell her that Alex is here,"

"She does prefer to have appointments, ma'am…"

"Do you think Kathy would like to lose a sale that will be in the neighborhood of 20,000 dollars? I'm an old client. Now get her," ordered Alex, fire lighting her pale blue eyes. Patty felt the anger as intense energy emanating from the hand that still held hers gently but firmly in its grasp.

"Alex, calm down. You're going to make yourself sick, " cautioned a worried Patty quietly.

"Sweetheart, I promise you I'm not the one who is going to be sick," Alex whispered back with a wide smile, stroking the golden head beside her.

"Oh…Um, shouldn't you have been nicer to that lady? Isn't she someone important?"

"No, she is a sales clerk. She's a snob; and it's my opinion that she should be an unemployed sales clerk. Kathy has a heart of gold, though, so she will probably just have a little chat with that viper. Maybe she will learn not to judge people then."

"I don't understand, Alex. She seemed like she was in charge."

"Unfortunately, there are some sales people who act like that, but Kathy owns this place, and I've known her for a long, long time. I'm one of her oldest and most frequent patrons. She is a sweetie, who is going to make you look like a princess…"

"Me?"

"Yep."

"But…."

"No buts. We are going home to an elegant dinner for two, and for that we need elegant attire. That's why we are here."

"Wow, really?"

"Yes, really."

"Wow."

Alex smiled and embraced the flustered young woman.

Suddenly Katherine Gardz, the designer and owner of the

shop, appeared at their side. She smiled at Alex and shook her head; "You certainly know how to scare the hell out of my staff, young lady."

Alex lifted an eyebrow and one hand went to her hip as she pulled slightly away from Patty, though she still had an arm around her shoulders. She couldn't seem to separate herself completely from the smaller woman. "Well, your staff shouldn't be so damn snobby, and I wouldn't have to scare some manners into them."

"Okay, okay, I'll talk to her. She's a bit new and not used to the clientele here yet. Come here, you brat, and give an old lady a hug."

Alex sighed inwardly but smiled and reluctantly let go of Patty so she could give her old friend a hug. Then she reached out and reclaimed a little hand to pull the smaller woman closer, "Kathy, this is Patty. I want you to make her even more beautiful then she already is, though I don't think that's possible since she's perfect. I also need a little something, but here's the difficult bit--I want the results to be a surprise for each of us. I don't want us to get a peep at each other until later, so we'll need separate fitters...nice fitters, especially for my little one here."

Katherine's eyebrow's shot up into her bangs. This was unprecedented in her long, long acquaintance with the young woman before her. Katherine was an older woman in her 60's, very attractive, and a friend of Alex's late mother. She'd known Alex all her life. First her mother and then her Uncle Vito took little Alex for every Christmas dress she'd ever had. She knew all of Alex's secrets and kept them proudly. She also knew that Alex had never bought any of her woman presents before. This was a first; She could clearly see the change in her young friend . Alexa was in love; and this sweet young girl didn't know it, but Katherine could see that the tall, stoic woman would do anything for the little blonde. Katherine knew this would please Alex's late mother, so she wanted to do anything she could to help the two young women . "I think we could manage that, but, Alex, in order for your plan to work, you will have to let go of her hand."

Alex lifted Patty's hand to her lips, kissed it gently on the palm, and then she let it go, "All right. I release this beautiful hand into your gentle custody. Make sure she is treated like a princess, Kathy, because to me, she is," said Alex fervently, her gaze never leaving Patty's, though she was talking to the older woman beside them. Patty was shedding a few tears, overwhelmed by the treatment she was receiving, "No tears, I want only smiles tonight," said Alex as she dried the tears and caressed the soft cheek.

Patty nodded and said in a scratchy voice, "Okay."

Katherine smiled at the interaction of obvious love between the two women. It was a relief for her to see this side of Alex again. It was rare to see the playful child of long ago in the stoic woman of today. She shed her facade so rarely, and yet, it was easy to see that Patty brought out that part of her with just her presence. "Ok, my shy young ward, let's go make you beautiful for Alex," she said as she led the blonde away.

"Like I said, you can't make her beautiful. There is no one on this earth more beautiful then she is," called Alex as she sat down on the satin couch waiting for her own fitter to come out and help her get ready for the most important night of her life.

*****

Alex had been helped by the head fitter while Katherine herself attended to Patty. A slue of boxes found their way into Alex's trunk, then she sped to their next stop. Patty was surprised to find herself in front of her own apartment, and she looked at the older woman in confusion. Alex smiled and caressed her shoulder, explaining quietly, " I would like it very much if you would spend the night at my place. I have a room all picked out for you, and I thought that maybe you would like to bring some of your things. I also know that Fluffy needs to be taken care of so she will be a happy kitty when you come home. In fact if you want to, you can bring Fluffy with you," Alex finished with the most endearing look that Patty had yet seen.

Patty threw her arms around Alex and hugged her tightly saying breathlessly, "Thank you. You are so sweet and thoughtful." Patty took the initiative for the first time and kissed Alex deeply.

Alex returned the kiss feeling quite giddy. She had made a promise to herself to go really slowly with Patty. She might have broken her first vow by kissing her, but she wasn't going to do anything further until the woman in her arms was ready for it. She enjoyed the tender kiss. She was glad she was doing this in the right way; she would do anything in her power to make this woman happy.

When they pulled back, Patty smiled at Alex and gently brushed some hair out of the enticing blue eyes as she asked, "Can I really bring Fluffy to your place?"

"Of course," replied Alex as she leaned into the gentle caress that her little love was giving her cheek as she spoke of the small white cat.

"Um...I don't want her to ruin any of your beautiful stuff. She is still a kitten and has a tendency to scratch, so...."

"I don't care if she scratches everything in the house. All I want is for you to be happy, and Fluffy makes you happy. Come on, let's go get your furry friend," she said as she unbuckled her belt and indicated that they should get a move on. *There's a lot to do, my love,* thought Alex as they got out of the car and headed up to Patty's apartment.

*****

When they got to Alex's, her staff was waiting to help the women with their purchases and Patty's things. Alex held Fluffy in her carrier in one hand and Patty's hand in the other as she led her charges into her home. She led them upstairs to a bedroom that two of her staff were just leaving, giving Alex a nod to let her know that all was ready. Alex smiled and nodded back as she gently set Fluffy down on the floor and turned to the blonde whose hand was still in her own. "Get dressed, sweetheart," she said in a barely heard whisper. Then she kissed Patty's cheek, let go of her hand and left the room, closing the door gently behind her.

Patty opened the carrier to let Fluffy out so she could explore her new room, deciding that her pet was not going to go outside of the bedroom. She didn't want to endanger any more furniture then necessary. Then she went to the bed where the first three boxes with all the clothing that she and Katherine had chosen were carefully placed. A fourth box, a small rectangular one, confused her; she had no idea what was inside of it. Opening it, she slowly sat down on the bed in shock. Inside the box were a necklace and earrings with perfectly matching emeralds. The green color matched her eyes perfectly. Patty, amazed, looked toward the door and quietly murmured in a very throaty whisper, "Oh, Alex."

*****

Alex was dressed in a cobalt blue evening gown. On each ear was a perfectly matched sapphire blue earring that made her eyes sparkle. Her hair was pulled up in a French twist that showed off her neck to perfection. She looked stunning and very, very nervous. This was her first ever attempt at real romance, and since this was the love of her life, she wanted to do it right.

She was pacing on the landing outside of Patty's room, waiting for her love to get dressed. She had just turned back toward the room for the 10th time when the door swung open and then quickly closed. Alex froze to the spot. Before her stood a vision in a blue-green off-the-shoulder evening gown with a slit up the right leg, showcasing that piece of shapely anatomy. She looked like the princess Alex had told Katherine she wanted her to be. Patty smiled shyly and twirled to give

Alex the full effect of the carefully selected ensemble.

"How do I look?" Patty asked, blushing, and then noting how stunning Alex looked, said, "Wow, you look amazing. God, I wish I looked like you."

"You don't know how glad I am you don't look like me, " said Alex as she slowly crossed to Patty and took her hand, She marveled for the hundredth time how well their hands seemed to just mold perfectly together. "God, Patty, you don't know how enchanting you look. You take my breath away. Come on, my love, let's enjoy our evening together."

They walked down to the first floor and instead of heading to the dining room, Alex led her companion to the verandah. Patty gasped. It looked like a wonderland, with little white Christmas lights strung everywhere. There were pink lights up and down the trellis, and the table was a picture in pink and white--beautifully done in antique china and red Florentine crystal glasses.

Now Patty felt slightly faint. Alex noticed her swaying and took her to a seat at once. She bent down and quietly whispered into her ear, "Do you like it?"

Patty just nodded her head, tears trickling down her cheeks. Alex knelt down and used a finger to gently wipe away a tear. "Tears? Are you...Did I..." Panic started to rise in Alex's throat in reaction to the unexpected display.

"No, no, Alex, These are happy tears."

Alex breathed a sigh of relief and hugged the small woman to her. "Oh, thank God." She backed up a bit so she could see Patty's face. "I wanted this to be so perfect and gentle and....and ...beautiful. More then anything, I want to see you smile. Am I asking too much?" Alex asked in an uncharacteristically shy voice.

Patty shook her head. "This is perfect. It's beyond my imagination. Thank you."

"Oh, sweetheart, it has not even begun yet," Alex said with a smile as she took her seat and rang the bell for dinner to be served.

Chapter Five
Murder

"Where is the music coming from, Alex?" They were sitting at the table finishing the meal with an incredible dessert that Alex's chef had spent all day concocting.

Alex smiled and pointed to the beam over the French doors, "Hidden speakers all along there. Are you done, Patty?" she asked with a breathtaking smile.

"Yes."

Would you like to dance with me?"

Patty's eyes sparkled. "Oh yes, That would be wonderful," she replied with a delighted laugh.

Alex stood up gracefully and presented Patty with her hand. Patty placed her hand in Alex's elegant one and was gently pulled to her feet, then Alex led her to a part of the verandah that was perfect for dancing. It was slightly raised and had a plethora of flowers and plants around it, making it appear enchanted to Patty's already lovesick gaze. As their arms entwined, Patty's hand fell naturally on Alex's broad shoulders. Alex pulled Patty close and laid her head on top of

Patty's, smelling her sweet scented hair.

Alex sighed. If she died right at that moment in time, she would be happy. This was the ultimate joy, except for what might be coming later. She tightened her hold and smiled dreamily. She was in no hurry. This was going to be at Patty's pace. She loved the way their relationship was developing--so peacefully, so easily. She felt so comfortable with the familiar young woman. No one in Alex's whole life had ever touched her very soul like this sweet, gentle beauty did, and she would wait a lifetime if that was what Patty needed.

*****

Patty was in the same dreamy and contented state as her companion. She simply could not believe that she was so incredibly happy. She felt that just she and Alex were floating on a beautiful cloud, totally excluding the rest of the world. Smiling as she felt Alex pull her into a tighter embrace, Patty felt so loved and protected in those strong arms--like a cocoon where no one could intrude.

*****

Suddenly Alex's butler stood at the doorway. He looked at his preoccupied mistress and cleared his throat once. Receiving no response from his employer, he frowned and cleared his throat louder, but still there was no reaction from the tall woman. He was quite puzzled. He had never seen her so distracted that she didn't acknowledge his discreet signal. Finally, he had no choice. He walked a little farther out onto the verandah and said quietly, "Ahem, Miss Alexandra."

Alex and Patty jumped, they were both so unaware of their surroundings.

Alex whirled on her old retainer "Damn it, how many times have I told you not to do that. You scared us." Though Alex's voice was calm, the man saw ice in those beautiful blue eyes that clearly bespoke her anger. She had an arm around Patty and she was gently rubbing her back to calm the frightened young woman. Her voice dropped an octave as she said to him, "I can't tolerate this type of intrusion. What is the reason for it?"

The butler stared at her for moment. She had never spoken to him in this way before. Never. Not even as a child had she treated him with anything but respect. Her parents had treated him poorly many times, but young Miss Alexandra treated all household members with dignity, He really must have displeased her to warrant such treatment, though he didn't understand how. "I apologize, Ma'am. You have an urgent phone call and I have been trying to get..."

"Who is the call from?" Her voice was still filled with annoyance.

"A Miss Val, Ma'am."

Alex cleared her throat. "Excuse me, Patty. Sip your coffee. I will be right back."

*****

She strode to the phone and picked it up in one long angry movement. "What!"

There was heavy breathing for a moment, then Val answered very quietly, "Robby is dead."

"What?" The tone of her voice was totally different, her disbelief dispelling the anger completely.

Val's voice quavered; it was breathless and distraught. "I don't know who took him out. The person was good, very good. No traces, no evidence, just Robby lying there in his own blood, dead. He was stabbed at close range. Alex, he was a rookie, but he was good. Who could have gotten close enough to do this? Did you change your mind?"

"Don't be ridiculous. I like Robby, I could never have done that. It goes against everything I stand for, This even goes against the family's ethics. What do the police think?"

"My contact says that it looks like a professional hit, and that poor Robby must have been dead for at least 8 hours. I ...I should have gone over when he didn't answer his page. Maybe if I had he'd still be..."

"Don't do that to yourself, Val. Let me think about this. Don't go home. Go to the safe house. I'll call you tomorrow after I figure our next move. Bye."

"Okay. Bye," was the quiet reply from the other end, followed by a dial tone.

Alex brought the phone to her chin and snarled her lips in anger. She shook her head to clear her thoughts.

She retraced her steps back to where Patty was waiting. How would she face her new friend, her new love, with this teeming inside her? She was so upset, and yet she wanted ...no...needed Patty near her. *Frustration to the left of me and frustration to the right of me. I'll just put this aside for now. I'll face it in the morning. The most important person in my life is waiting for me, and I won't disappoint her or myself.*

Patty was gazing at the stars, her head slightly tilted back. To Alex's loving eyes, she sparkled more then the brightest star.

"Hi," Alex said, smiling down at the beauty before her.

"Oh...hi." She stuttered a bit, startled, " Sorry I guess my mind was a million miles away. It is beautiful here, isn't it?"

Alex's eyes never left Patty. "Yes, very beautiful," she replied quietly.

Patty blushed fiercely as she realized that Alex was talking about her.

"Red becomes you," Alex teased. "Come on, let's continue our dance. We won't be interrupted anymore." Alex guided her back to the verandah where they had danced earlier. Now they were dancing again, slowly and sensuously. They became entranced by each other's rhythm, and the feel of the other's skin. Hands were exploring backs, and Alex lowered her head and kissed Patty's neck. Slowly an earlobe found its way between Alex's perfect white teeth. Within the trance that held them both captive, two heads slowly lifted 'til eyes met. Patty nodded, and they silently left the patio, hand in hand.

*****

They entered Alex's master bedroom quietly and Alex shut the door. They couldn't seem to gaze deeply enough into each other's eyes as they were drawn into a sweet embrace. Lowering her head, Alex kissed Patty passionately. Patty was so deeply drawn into the kiss she didn't even feel herself being lifted into Alex's arms. Alex wasn't sure how they had gotten on the bed, but she cuddled the smaller woman and whispered into Patty's ear.

"Nothing is going to happen here that you don't want, my love. All the shots will be called by these lips," She kissed Patty again deeply, and when they came up for air she continued hoarsely, her voice full of passion, "I will follow your lead."

Blue eyes delved into green and awaited the next decision. The trust and hope in Alex's eyes nearly broke Patty's heart. She snuggled Alex's neck and whispered back softly, "I want you to teach me how to love you, Alex. I don't know how to lead because I don't know what to do."

Alex smiled gently and kissed Patty's forehead as she replied. "I know this, but I don't want to scare you or overwhelm you, little one. I want it to be beautiful. We will go very slowly..."

"I don't want to bore you, Alex. I'm sure you have more urgent needs..."

"I only need two things. I need your love, and I need to make you happy. That's all. Oh, my love, you are far too exciting to ever bore me. Why would you think that?" Alex asked as she gently kissed Patty's nose, then each eye and then nibbled her ear, awaiting a reply.

Patty couldn't breathe for a moment, much less answer. Each time this woman touched her, she felt she would explode from the pleasure of the contact.

Alex nuzzled her neck as she said, "Patty, you are a very exciting woman, and I want you so badly I can hardly breathe. But please, my darling, tell me what you need."

"You," Patty answered in a hoarse whisper. "I need you. I want to please you. " She started to kiss Alex's neck with delightful little butterfly kisses that inflamed Alex's body. She arched her neck in pleasure and just let the young woman explore. Slowly Patty descended down to Alex's breasts, but found what she most wanted to taste was encased in the sexy dress that Alex still wore. She made an unsuccessful attempt to remove it and delighted Alex with her tiny cat like growl of frustration.

With a mischievous smile Alex said, "I'll help you, if you'll help me."

"Deal."

Slowly both woman undressed themselves giving each other a bit of show that further inflamed them. When they were both bare, they smiled simultaneously and said, "Beautiful."

Chuckling, Alex said, "Two great minds with but a single thought." Then Alex brought her head down to Patty's breast and gave it the attention it desired. Slowly, naturally, they explored and loved each other's bodies 'til Patty's moment of decision came.

Alex's eyes, dark with desire, looked deeply into Patty's. They were hooded and glazed. Alex voice was just barely a whisper as she asked gently, "Are you ready, my love?"

Patty nodded and smiled, trust radiated from her, and Alex cherished and deflowered her with such gentle love that they both came in the same timeless moment.

Once they calmed, Alex cradled Patty in her arms and asked, "Are you all right, sweetheart?"

Patty nodded her head.

"Will I hear your voice ever again?"

Patty laughed gently and said in dreamy whisper, "I love

you, Alexandra Bennet."

Alex had tears in her eyes as she replied, "I love you with all my heart, Patricia Darcy." She lowered her head and kissed her with a need deeper then she even knew that she had. She knew that this girl was her soul mate and her home.

*****

The next morning Alex woke up curled around the woman she loved and cherished. She held her tightly and thought about how she was going to protect this precious woman from the vendetta she knew was coming. Robby's death had been meant as warning, a calling card to her. She felt it in her soul. The only way to really protect Patty was to never see her again. At the very thought, a darkness fell upon her, choking her, and a tight, death like grip squeezed her heart. She felt the effect of it to such a degree that she knew if she pushed Patty away, she would die.

No, separation is not an option, Alex, she thought to herself as she bent down and kissed a golden eyebrow, causing its owner to wiggle slightly but not awaken. *How do I protect you, my sweet? How do I protect us?* Alex took a deep breath. She nuzzled her love's hair, breathing in the sweet fragrance as she considered carefully. *There is only one way: I have to find out who is behind this and stop it before it starts. But is it too dangerous? Too elaborate?*

Suddenly Alex was distracted by sweet little kisses between her breasts, up her neck to her chin. She opened her eyes to find deep emerald orbs looking back at her.

"That's better," Patty said at Alex's delighted smile.

"What?"

"You looked so sad. I just wanted to make you smile."

"Well, my love, you found a delightful way to draw it out. Okay, it is Saturday. What would be your pleasure on this beautiful day? We have no plans and no work today; and since I love you so much, I'm going to let you choose."

"Oh gosh, I've never had a weekend off. I wouldn't even know what to choose. You do it this time, my love, and then I will next time, okay?"

Alex sighed deeply and then pulled Patty into a firm embrace, "To tell you the truth, I would love to just stay in bed cuddling with you all day."

Patty kissed Alex's cheek and snuggled into Alex's warm hold. "Wouldn't that be a bit boring for you, Alex?"

"With you? Never! Patty, why do you keep saying that?" Alex lifted her head so she could see into her love's eyes.

"Until I met you, Alex... I never had anyone say I was anything wonderful like you do. Not beautiful or attractive or exciting or even fun. You are the first person who ever said any of that to me. I guess it's kind of new...I'm sorry...I...."

"Shhh, Don't apologize, my love. It's not your fault you were involved with such blind stupid people. You are all those things and so much more. I am intoxicated by you. Just seeing you makes my heart pump faster. Touching you and having you in my arms is beyond heavenly. You are so special, my love, it is beyond my ability to describe it." Alex smiled at the deep blush that quickly spread over the blonde's entire body. Alex started to kiss and taste her until she was writhing in pleasure. "Oh my, Patty, I think you are now my favorite breakfast. Let's have seconds." Alex slowly went over the edge, and took her lover happily with her.

*****

Alex was in her office at the mansion completely engrossed in the computer. Patty was in her den on another computer, working on sales homework Peter had given her. Alex was going through her exclusive files trying to figure out who had killed Robby. The phone rang and she grimaced. "Who the hell is calling me at home on Saturday afternoon?' she said to the ringing instrument before she reached for the receiver.

"Yes?" she said briskly into black instrument.

"Alex, it's Val..."

"Valerie, god damn it, I told you to go to the safe house and maintain silence until I contacted you. Why the hell..."

"Alex, I am at the safe house. I just wanted... I ...well, I think I remembered something from Robby's apartment that might help."

Alex looked kind of sheepish. Her tone changed into one of interested inquiry. "What did you remember, Val?" "When I looked at the rug next to Robby's body, there was some extra red. Now that I think about it, it wasn't blood. It was something else, some kind of a designed shape, like the letter Z."

"The letter Z? What do you think...Wait a minute, you don't think that it's..."

"Alex, do you know for sure that Zarrelli is dead?"

Alex stared at the black receiver in her hand like she didn't know how it got there. "No, Val I don't. You stay put. I mean it, Val--don't move. I don't want you looking into this. Don't call anyone else, I mean it, Don't even call your mother. Don't call me or Vito. I will call you, and from now on, only on the scrambler."

"I want to help, Alex. I need to. For Robby. Besides, if it is Franco, this is serious shit. I know you're good, but you can't do this on your own. This will be deadly."

"You said it, my friend. I'll be in touch. Ciao, Val."

"Ciao, Alex, Be careful."

Alex hung up and stared sightlessly at the computer. Franco Zarrelli was an ex-partner of her father's. Her father'd had him dispatched after a botched coup was discovered to have been his doing. Alex and her father were to be the victims of a car bomb in Alex's beloved Porsche. It was only discovered in time because Alex couldn't get her CD player to play without a strange metallic sound. Her dad figured out what it was in time to save their lives, but Alex lost her beautiful car to the explosion.

The Zarrelli's yacht was blown to bits in retaliation, with

the entire family believed to be aboard. At least that's what Alex's dad had thought at the time. If not, then there was one of three people it could be--Franco, his son Tomas, or his daughter Julia.

This information could be deadly for Alex, Vito, Val and now...Patty.

"Damn," said Alex to her reflection in the computer monitor.

*****

Patty knocked gently at Alex's office door. Alex's head snapped up, and her worried face transformed into one of delight. Just seeing Patty before her calmed and soothed her soul. It didn't solve the problem, and it certainly didn't make it go away, but her love was safe and with her. And that was all that mattered.

"You all finished with your homework, young lady? Do you want me to check it for you?" she asked with a mischievous smile.

Patty's smile matched Alex's, "Yes, Mom. Make sure I get an A. Okay?"

Alex shook her head and tilted it. "Believe me, my love, maternal is not a way to describe how I feel about you."

"Yeah, I know...Thank God, huh? Alex, are you okay? You looked really upset when I came in, " Patty said as she slipped a protective arm around Alex's shoulders. Alex felt warmed by the gesture, and she didn't want to lie so she used the old standby dodge. " I'm okay sweetheart. Just some business worries. You know how it is when you run a company as big as mine--even on Saturday I get hit in the face with them. Um... Patty, when you got the tour around the office did you notice any redheads? I mean Raggedy Ann red?"

Patty was a little startled by the sudden change of subject. "Wh... a man or woman?"

"Either." The Zarrelli family had only one common trait--

natural bright red hair that they were all incredibly proud of; so it was doubtful they would cover it up or dye it. Their ego wouldn't let them. Peter had given Patty a tour of the facility the day before, and she was bright and observing, It was a shot in the dark, but Alex was hopeful that her intelligent lover would have noticed one of the Zarrelli's if they had been there.

Patty sat on the edge of the desk with her arms crossed. She was still confused, but she answered the question as well as she could. "There were two. One was a man, an engineer; and the other was a woman, Peter's new secretary. She and I both had to go through all the training yesterday. Why, Alex?"

Hmm, two positions that could have heard of Robby's mistake through the gossip mill, if they were nosy enough. I'll have to tighten security and look into these two. Especially Peter's new secretary. Only a nice looking woman could have gotten that close to Robby. She smiled, and out loud said, "I have some concerns about espionage. Software is vulnerable to that sort of thing, and I had a tip today that it might be happening. I thought with your talented eyes you might have noticed something. And, of course, you did," she finished with a grin. She reached up and pulled Patty into her lap and kissed and hugged her with gratitude. She felt bad about ending up with a lie, but Patty just didn't need to know about the potential danger they were all in. Alex's goal in life was to protect her, and that's what she was going to do.

Alex pulled back slightly and tilted the woman's head up so she could see her beautiful eyes, "Now, would you like to do something fun?"

"Yes, What do you have in mind?"

"Do you swim?'

"You mean in the indoor pool you showed me?"

"Yes, but you didn't answer my question."

"Of course I swim, Alex. It sounds like fun, let's go," she replied excitedly, pulling the older woman behind her.

Alex had big bright smile on her face for two reasons. The first was that she had succeeded in distracting her love from the problem she was getting interested in. The second reason brightened Alex's smile even more--it was the thought of skinny dipping with the beautiful woman pulling her towards her pool. *When life is good, it's very, very good,* Alex thought to herself as she followed Patty down the hall

Chapter Six

Confessions

One naked, wet blonde was definitely taking Alex's mind off her troubles. She watched as the golden haired beauty frolicked in the water like a skilled dolphin. A sudden urge sent Alex under the water, seeking her beautiful preys lovely legs. She gently grabbed a leg and then climbed seductively up the shapely body until she embraced Patty in long arms. They surfaced to take a deep breath, looked longingly into each other eyes, and then submerged again as their lips met in an erotic, passionate kiss.

When they next surfaced, deep breaths were essential; but neither woman objected since it added to the visual for both.

"You are so beautiful, Patty," Alex said as she cupped Patty's cheeks in her elegant palms.

"I am?" Green eyes looked into blue, full of vulnerable need. The two women moved to sit on the top step of the pool. "My darling, you are the most beautiful, precious part of my life. Umm, Patty...all I want is for you to be happy and safe...I..."

Two wet, naked bodies sank into a mutual embrace as Patty

answered Alex's declaration,. "I love you Alex. I don't think I've ever felt like this before. Oh God, Alex...,"she moaned as Alex kissed her again.

"Thank you, my love. I don't think, I know that I have never felt this way in my life. Patty, will you stay with me?"

Patty looked confused. "Alex, I am staying with you."

"No, Patty...I mean, forever?" Alex was completely open and vulnerable at that moment. She knew that with one word Patty could devastate her, but she also knew that she couldn't live without having this special young woman in her life every day from now on.

"I would be honored to, but why me?"

Alex's eyes filled with tears of joy and grief. "My love, I...God, how can I explain...I never really thought I could feel this deeply. I need you, I love you. You inspire me to want to be a better person...I..." Alex was sobbing uncontrollably now. Patty threw her arms around her and held the tall woman as closely as she could. She gently rubbed her back and kissed her cheek and neck. Slowly they parted, and Alex took a deep breath and looked deeply into Patty's eyes as she came to a decision. She quietly rose and said, "Get your robe on, my love. I don't want you giving your answer to my invitation 'til we go to my office and discuss a few things.

*****

They were now both dressed in jeans and Tee shirts as they entered Alex's office, their hair still wet from their swim.

"Please have a seat." Patty went to sit in one of the visitor's chairs. "No Patty, please sit here in my chair." Alex waited until the smaller woman was comfortably seated, then she started to pace.

"Patty, you know all about Toys Inc. and our facilities, right?" Patty nodded, unable to follow what her lover was trying to tell her. "Well, what I'm about to reveal to you may end all your feelings for me, but I really need to be honest because I love you so very much. I need you to see who and what I really am. We all wear masks, Patty, and my mask covers some very ugly things. I need you to know what your getting into before you answer the question I posed at the pool."

She reached over Patty's shoulder and called up a coded documents file marked MI. Then she selected three sub-documents within it and enlarged them for the girl to read.

"Okay, Patty, read this one first, then the second and the third. Then, my love, you'll know all of me. Not just the executive or your lover, but my hidden darker side, my demons. It's not a very pretty sight to see, I assure you. I'm going to give you some privacy now. I'll be in my room making some phone calls. If you want to get the hell out of here after you've read this, I will understand. If you want to talk...well then, we'll talk. I can't sit here and watch you read this; it would...kill me..." There were tears falling from Alex's eyes, and before Patty could react, the dark haired beauty was gone--unable to watch the love of her life read the horrors she'd perpetrated in her past.

Alex called Vito to make arrangements to find out a little more about their assassin, masquerading in the guise of Peter's secretary. She then called Val to make sure she was following instructions; and, finally, she took her tea and sank into the deep white chair by the large picture window in her bedroom. She was miserable, but she'd had to do what she did for Patty's sake. She couldn't keep her in the dark any longer. She knew if the girl ran, as she should, that she would let her go. She also knew that this new Alex would be left an empty shell. She couldn't be the head of Murder Inc. anymore, but she didn't know if she would even be able to function on a daily basis without Patty in her day. *It's strange: I was on the path to my old self, but finding Patty pushed the envelope, and now I don't know what I'll do without her love. I'm a survivor, so I will find a way; but I may die of unhappiness*, she thought morosely as she sipped her tea.

She didn't hear the quiet entry of the other woman. Patty stood in the doorway looking at the forlorn visage before her. She'd felt several emotions at once while she was reading the documents in Alex's office: anger, fear, betrayal, love, compassion and sympathy. Love had won, and as she looked at the expression of utter misery on the face of the woman she loved, she knew it was the right choice. While she was reading, betrayal and compassion seemed to be fighting a battle within her own mind. Now as she stood watching this sad, special woman, it was love and sympathy for all that she had gone through, and what she had come to mean to her already, that was causing her heart to beat faster. She couldn't leave her, even if she wanted to; and she didn't want to.

"Alex?"

Alex turned. Her eyes were red and she had a look of disbelief on her face. "You're still here?"

"Yes."

"Why?"

"Because, above all else I love you with all my heart I am hurt that you deceived me before, and I'm scared by the things that you did for your father...but I do trust you now. Even after reading all that horror you caused, because I know that you're not that person anymore. I don't think you ever were. Your father manipulated you into that position, and then you just followed his instructions. I think when he was killed, your grief made you blind with rage; and that you've now recovered. I really don't think you have been that killer for a long time. The last paper told me what I really needed to know."

"You mean the letter of intent?"

Patty nodded and walked to the edge of Alex's bed. "Did you decide to give up that...company..." Patty couldn't hide her contempt for all Murder Inc. stood for, "before or after you met me?"

"Both." Alex sighed and closed her tired, red rimmed eyes. "I never wanted it, but my Father made sure I would follow through by convincing Vito that he couldn't. Like you said, when Dad was killed...I...lost it, " she said in a small, distant voice; and Patty could see, for just a moment, that scared little girl that Alex had been. Wild, deserted, and very alone.

"That was the vendetta detailed in the first document?" Patty was outraged and scared by Alex's own calm description of her grief and rage, which became the cruel erasing of a whole crime family. It was like a page from some horrible crime novel, but this was true life and Alex did it.

"Yes. I was not even human. I lost my heart. All I could feel were anger and hate." She looked at Patty with a deep tormented grief in her sad eyes and said, "Vito reminded me of who I really was after it was all over. It was Vito who grabbed me and said stop. He is the only person in my life at the time who could have done that. He was the only soul since my Mother passed who ever saw my heart...'til you, my love. Did you read the second document?"

Patty nodded, "That man that shot at me worked for you, and now he's dead, and you were saying how worried you are about us all."

"Yes. If I had a brain in my head, that incident would have convinced me to make you stay as far away from me as you can, so you would be safe."

"Funny, I think your concern for all of us in that document is what convinced me not to run. I've got to tell you, Alex, that after I read that, I almost ran screaming out of this house. I almost ran like a bat out of hell. You scared me. I couldn't believe that the same woman that I was in love with could be so vicious. That the woman who was so gentle with me, could kill so easily. But I stayed. I had to see the connection between the woman you were and the woman you are now. So I stayed and read on. As I saw you change in the documents, I became calmer and calmer. That third one told me I have to..."

"No, Patty, you don't have to."

Patty got up and walked over to the seated woman. She sat on the edge of the chair, put both arms around her neck, and said, "Yes, I do. I have to stay and be with you. I need to show you that I see the real you, too. You see, Alexandra Bennett, I am hopelessly in love with you. I always knew there was something...hidden and dark. I felt it twice, very strongly. The first time was when you confronted my boss at the cappuccino stand, and you practically had him sweating in a panic just by looking at him. The second was the night that phone call interrupted our dance. I see the flashes of worry and sadness all the time; I am not blind. Now I know it's deeper then I ever imagined; it's not profit or greed, it's life and death. I think, my love, that you're on the verge of changing your life; and I very much want to be a part of that."

Alex's blue eyes were filled with tears that slowly tracked down her cheeks; She put her head on Patty's shoulder as she replied very softly, "Please, my little love, be very careful. This verge is on a pinnacle, and we could both plunge to our deaths."

Patty gently rested her head on top of Alex's "I know that, Alex, Remember before, you said you need me?" She felt Alex nod her head against her shoulder. "Well, I need you, too. We'll stay balanced on that pinnacle because we have each other. That's what soul mates do, they stand by your side to the foot of the gallows and beyond."

At those words, Alex just fell apart. She started sobbing, but she knew that they were healing tears, and that Patty was the reason for them. She couldn't believe the amount of faith that Patty had in her, but she vowed in her heart to try her best not to fail her beloved.

*****

Patty and Alex were seated in the kitchen. Except for the cook who prepared all their meals in the morning, the rest of the staff had the day off. The two women now completely alone in the house, alone together for the first time since they were in Patty's apartment. They were both just as nervous as they had been that first time, even if it was for a completely different reason.

They were both silently eating sandwiches that the cook had left them, so filled with emotions and thoughts that words didn't seem to be able to pass their lips. Shame and sorrow swallowed every word that tried to get past Alex's lips; she couldn't seem to get through that wall that she herself had built.

Finally Patty had to say what was on her mind, "Can I answer your request now?" Confused, Alex looked up from the food she was playing with and replied, "What request?"

Patty smiled gently. "Have you forgotten your request by the pool so soon?"

Alex blushed closed her eyes and shook her head. She didn't look up at Patty again.

"Alex?"

"Yes?"

"Yes."

"Yes, what?"

"What do you think?"

Alex slowly looked up again and saw a vision of calm, dignified determination before her. "Yes? But why... I mean, my God, Patty, I'm not exactly a good risk."

Patty shook her head, "How little you know yourself. Sheesh, Alex, you were already slowly changing yourself through Toys Inc. long before you met me. You have already separated yourself emotionally from that dark world. Now, without any help, you're doing it legally and physically. I'd say that is a person I should invest in. .. Besides, I'm helplessly in love with you, and I want to be with you...forever." Patty walked around the table and gently brought tear-filled eyes up to meet her own and added, "If you still want me."

Arms reached around Patty and drew her into a tight emotional embrace. "Want you? Of course I want you! God knows how much I love you. You are so damned special. I can't believe that you still want me. I am amazed...You are...a miracle." She brought the sweet lips to her own and kissed the woman she loved.

"No, I'm not a miracle," Patty replied as they parted slightly. "I'm just the one who was lucky enough to be in the wrong place at the right time, and I had my own avenging angel to save me from her own man's stupid mistake. God, I'm just so very, very lucky."

"No. I'm lucky. I was lucky enough to find you, then save your life. Do you really want to?"

"Oh, Alex; and you say I need help with my ego."

Alex smiled and kissed her forehead gently, then shifted ever so gracefully, pulling the smaller woman onto her lap, "I'm only vulnerable with you because I love you so very much. That's when I knew that you were the one. I felt so vulnerable. I cared what you thought of me from the very beginning. I'd never felt that way with anyone else before. Only you brought that out in me, my love, only you. I want…no, I need…I …Patty, promise you will stay with me forever. Please? "

Patty kissed Alex deeply, then she kissed her neck, then caressed her cheek as she said quietly, "Life's funny. You are the first person in my life since my Grandma that didn't see me as a figure of weakness. She always made me feel so special, just like you do. I feel invincible with you. Weird, huh?"

Alex interrupted nibbling a delicate ear to reply softly, " Very weird." Her voice was hoarse with passion as she rose with the petite woman in her arms. "May we continue this discussion somewhere more comfortable?"

*****

Two figures were peacefully sleeping in Alex's sun drenched living room. They were lying on the floor on a deep faux fur rug, cuddling contentedly in each other's arms.

Alex felt sweet little kisses between her breasts, and she smiled joyfully at the smaller woman. She opened one sky blue eye and her vision was filled with vibrant green.

"Hi."

"Hi. What time is it?"

"Eight p.m."

"Well, it was an interesting day, wasn't it?" Alex commented drolly.

"Yep, are you hungry?"

"Not really, I could just lie here with you forever...But I can hear the gentle rumblings of your tummy, so let's go feed you."

"Rumblings?"

A huge smile spread across Patty's face as she felt Alex kiss her way down to her tummy. Then the executive put her head next to it and looked up with a wicked gleam in her twinkling blue eyes. "Yep. I'd guess it's the Anvil Chorus."

Patty started to laugh, making Alex's head bounce, and the dark haired woman laughed with her in utter delight. *This is so wonderful. Damn, who would have thought my horrible confession would have brought us closer together. I never thought it could, but Patty's so loving. She loves me despite all my faults. I don't think I have ever felt closer to another living soul in my whole life.* She looked up at the laughing blonde, and her smile widened even more.

"Come on, let's feed the musicians."

*****

Alex and Patty were once again in the kitchen, this time eating cheesecake. Alex looked at Patty with what could only be described as a soulful expression "I think I like this meal better than the last one."

Patty's eyes twinkled at her as she replied, "Me, too. I love cheesecake!" A napkin landed neatly on her face. "Nice. This is not a good example of your table manners," Patty teased with a smirk.

"Oh, dear, and is there a punishment for this lack of decorum?"

"Well, I could deny you the pleasure of my attentions, but

that would punish me as much as it would you."

Alex's face suddenly turned serious. "No. That would be a true punishment, Patty."

"For me, too. I wouldn't do it," she replied just as seriously. "Alex, let's not get serious, please. I want to be silly, okay? There's more than enough serious stuff ahead of us."

"You're right." With that simple reply, Alex swept a squealing Patty into her arms and carried her upstairs to enjoy a more comfortable surrounding for being silly.

*****

Alex couldn't sleep. She'd made arrangements to set up the trap for Zarrelli, and then took the day off for Patty and herself. She knew there were only two things she could do when sleep failed her--work out, or bake--her only culinary skill. She slipped out of the blonde's embrace and went down to her kitchen. The workout room was next door to her bedroom, and she didn't want to wake her little love.

*****

When Patty's eyes opened, she saw a sea of pastries, a huge bright smile and pale blue eyes that were lit from within. She blinked her eyes a few times and asked huskily,"What's all this?"

"I must have made them wrong if you can't tell."

"Ha-Ha. Cute, Alex. Wait, you made this?"

Alex's smile brightened even more and she answered with pride in her voice, "Yep, I sure did."

"Wow!" The green eyes widened in surprise. "You're full of surprises. They look delicious."

"They are. Here try one, please?"

"Pick one for me."

Alex chuckled and picked a chocolate éclair, knowing

Patty's weakness for anything with chocolate. "This one?"

Patty had a mischievous urge, which she decided to follow, "Feed it to me, please," she requested, with a puckish smile on her face.

Alex looked astonished, then delighted, "Oh yes, my queen. We cannot allow your delicate hands to be sullied with chocolate, now can we?" replied the amazed Alex as she held the éclair close to Patty's already sweet lips.

Patty took a huge bite, and the raspberry jam mixed with the chocolate pastry in her mouth in delightful combination. Alex was intrigued by the delightful tongue that kept popping out of her lover's mouth to wipe up the remnants.

Hmm, let's test this most intriguing theory of mine, shall we? she thought to herself as she held out the pastry for the young blonde to take another bite. "Another bite, my queen?"

"Oh yes, my drop dead gorgeous serving wench. Mmm. It's very good, Alex, delicious in fact." Patty took another bite and the little tongue poked out again, causing the smile to widen on the already delighted face of the dark haired woman.

Oh yes, it will happen every time. Well good. I think it's time to enjoy the rewards of my little discovery.

"Last piece, my queen," she said out loud.

"Only of this one, right?"

"Oh yeah. Here, finish it so I can wipe my hands." She offered the last piece and quickly wiped her hands, watching Patty's mouth carefully. She leaned in closer, and when the little pink tongue popped out of the sweet mouth, Alex quickly sucked it into her own. Once captured, Patty gasped, then she sank into the delightful sensation. The game became a gentle exploration, developing into a passionate, deeply connected kiss.

When they parted for a breath, Patty said with a wide smile, "If we continue this way, I won't get any more goodies."

"Oh, my darling, don't worry. I think you'll get all the goodies you desire."

*****

"NO, DAMN IT!! Valerie I will not allow you to leave the safe house!" Alex yelled into the phone in her office on the second floor of her mansion.

"Come on, Alex, You need my help. I..."

"I do not!" Alex's voice was so loud that Patty could hear her clearly downstairs in the kitchen. The phone had interrupted breakfast, and that put the raven-haired woman into bad mood before she even picked up the receiver. Now Alex was seething as she paced back and forth in front of her speakerphone like a panther prowling its territory in search of intruders.

"I am not alone. I am also quite capable of handling this without your help. Now, you will stay put and stop arguing with me, or I will have you restrained. Got me?" she growled angrily into the phone.

Patty was now in the hallway, just out of sight. She waited for the appropriate moment to enter the room to see if she could prevent the woman she loved from giving herself a heart attack.

"I care, Alex," Val replied quietly through the speaker.

Alex stopped dead in her tracks and looked at the phone, losing some of the anger in acknowledgment of Val's words.

"I know you do, Val, but why be foolhardy," she replied to her employee, less harshly then she had before.

Patty breathed a sigh of relief at the reduction in anger she heard as she popped her head around the edge of the door, making herself suddenly visible to the taller woman.

Alex saw her immediately and motioned her in. Patty sat in one of the visitor chairs as she watched Alex continue her pacing.

"Then I guess I'm a fool. Alex, Robby didn't deserve to die."

"Who does, my friend? Remember what your profession is? You are an assassin. Val, I already have the beginnings of a vendetta on my hands. Let me handle this my own way; maybe I can prevent more bloodshed. You think you can do that for me? Please?" Her request was asked intently, her eyes in a blaze of passion as she stared at the instrument on her desk.

"I guess you're right. You are the boss."

"Damn straight. I'll be in touch. Goodbye, Val."

"Goodbye, Alex," Then a dial tone was heard.

Alex took a deep breath as she walked over to turn off her speakerphone. She looked at the woman in her visitor's chair sadly. "I'm sorry, Patty. I...my anger was caused by pure fear. I will not let anyone be killed by this maniac. Val is just too hot headed..."

Patty grinned impishly. "And you're not, love?"

Alex smiled and nodded in acknowledgment. "You're right, sweetheart. I am just as hot headed as she is. Are you mad at me?" she asked her soul mate in open vulnerability.

"No, I was just worried about you. I heard you yelling all the way in the kitchen, and I was afraid you'd give yourself a heart attack."

"Instead of being killed by a bullet, you mean?"

"Alex, I don't want you to die at all. I can't help it. Just like you need to protect me, I have that same driving need to protect you. Could we continue our nice peaceful mini vacation, or does that phone call end it?"

"I have taken the day off and so have you. Peter will start training you in accounting tomorrow. I need to...I am having a surveillance unit set up in Peter's office tonight, and I don't want you anywhere near there until I can see everything that goes on in that office."

"You don't think Peter...?"

"No, I do trust Peter. It's that new secretary of his that you told me about that I don't trust. I think she is the one that killed Robby. Only a woman could have gotten that close. And if it's her, you are in danger. It was very obvious last week how I feel about you. It makes you a...."

"A possible target?" Patty asked in squeaky voice.

"Yes," Alex replied, lowering her head.

Patty got up and put her arms around Alex's waist and rested her head on her chest. Alex's arms automatically went around Patty's waist protectively, and her head went on top of Patty's, satisfying her physical need to protect her love.

Quietly Patty spoke into Alex's chest, but Alex heard each word clearly. "I think I understand you fully now, Alex...God...I'm overwhelmed by your love, and my own need for you. Please...don't allow yourself to be killed because of me. I couldn't bear it.."

"I don't intend for anyone else to die. This will end soon, my love. Vito signs the papers tomorrow, and we'll start the transfer of operations for MI immediately. Hey, I really want you to meet Uncle Vito. He already likes you, and he hasn't even met you yet."

"I already like him, too, because he loves you so completely. I want to meet him very much." Patty looked up into warm blue eyes, she smiled and continued. "Since business is now complete, can we continue our playtime?"

"Oh yeah!" Alex's eyes twinkled at the thought of the kind of play that she had in mind. "Let the loving begin."

*****

They were on the deck of the outdoor pool area, lying side by side, their hands entwined and enjoying the feel of sun on their tired bodies.

"Alex?"

"Yes?"

"Can we get a puppy? Fluffy needs a playmate."

A dark head popped up. "A puppy?"

"Uh-huh."

"Why?"

Now the blonde's head popped up and green eyes met blue, "You need something to lavish all that love on."

78

"I have you for that."

Patty smiled brightly at her love as she continued, "Someone besides me. A soft vulnerable puppy, full of love just for you, like I have Fluffy who is totally loyal to me. You need a pet that can give you unconditional love and devotion. I think it would be a very good outlet for you."

"But, my love, you've already given me unconditional love. Isn't that enough?"

"Nope. Besides, I want a puppy too!"

"Who says I want it?"

Patty locked eyes with Alex's vibrant blue ones just above her. Alex laughed and kissed her deeply. When they parted she said quietly, "Okay, we'll go puppy hunting after work tomorrow."

Patty beamed. "No breeders. We get the puppy at the pound. Time to save another life, Alex."

Alex eyebrow rose. "Another life?"

"Well, you saved mine and Val's by keeping her at your safe house. I think the puppy would be a good addition to that. Don't you?"

"You are a very sneaky psychologist, my love. I guess I'll concede this argument though. We'll get the puppy at the pound tomorrow. Well, let's see--that's one puppy, and we already have a kitten; would you like anything else in our home?"

"Only you," Patty said, lowering her head onto Alex's shoulder.

"But you already have me, "Alex replied, kissing her forehead. "Is there anything you've always wanted?" Alex had had her butler go to Patty's apartment with a list of things to bring over for immediate use. They would be moving the golden haired woman into the mansion completely next weekend.

"Nope, I feel quite content."

Alex sighed and tightened her hold on the smaller woman in her arms, "So do I."

Chapter Seven
Trouble

Peter was pacing in Tommy's office waiting for an impromptu meeting with his boss. "Tommy, do you know what this is all about?"

"Yes. Relax, Peter, you're not in trouble," replied Tommy, gesturing to a chair in the visitors area.

"Then why am I locked out of my office?"

"For a very good reason, my friend," said Alex, entering with Patty by her side. "Tommy, would you take Patty to Accounting, She has a training session there this morning?"

Tommy nodded and smiled at Patty. "After you, Miss Darcy."

Patty rolled her eyes at Tommy. They were becoming good friends. "Drop the formality, old man, and lead the way," she replied with a smirk.

"See you later, smart Alec," Alex said with a grin.

"Bye, boss," Patty replied with a gentle caress of Alex's arm.

Alex watched them leave and then gestured for Peter to go into her office. She closed the door and motioned for the nervous man to settle into one of the visitor's chairs. Once he was seated, Alex sat on the edge of her desk and crossed her arms. "We've had a breech of security in MI, Peter. I'm afraid it came from Toys. That is more upsetting for me than I can say, I assure you. The worst of it is that it's in your department. I'm not upset with you, Peter, I'm protecting you."

Peter's eyes got wider and wider as Alex spoke. He stuttered a single word in reply. "Who?"

"Your new secretary. She's...shall we say ...she's not who she appears to be. You can't be blamed; she's very good. We need to string her along so I can put a surveillance unit in your office..."

"Wait, Alex if she's not...then who is she?"

Alex looked compassionately at her friend and trusted employee. "An assassin who killed one of my people."

Peter went very pale. "You mean Robby was killed by...?"

"Fraid so, my friend. Don't worry; she won't get away with it." There was an angry glint in Alex's eyes.

Peter swallowed and then quietly asked, "What are you going to do?"

"Set her up and then go in and sweep out all of her people. I will not have my reign end with a vendetta. I promised I wouldn't, and I won't," Alex replied, her voice full of conviction.

Shit, thought Peter angrily to himself, *What I have done by hiring this woman?*

Peter was pacing in front of Alex as he struggled with what she had just told him. Alex's blue eyes followed him in quiet sympathy. She knew he felt badly, but she was determined that he understand that this was not something he could have prevented.

"Peter, calm down, please. Everything is going to be okay."

"Calm down? It'll be okay? How the hell can you say that, Alex? I hired an assassin! Your enemy, for God's sake! I'm so sorry; you've always been so good and supportive of me, and then I go and, and..."

Alex couldn't stand watching this innocent man crumble right in front of her. "Shhh, stop now." She got up and led him to a guest chair, then knelt next to him so she was at his eye level. Looking deeply into his worried eyes, she said, "Now calm down. You could not have known about her. This is really very unusual, isn't it? You know that. We both know that there was not a single way for you to have known who she was. So, why this desperate need to blame yourself? Please stop projecting yourself into this mess, Peter. It started a very long time ago, and it has nothing whatsoever to do with you."

"Then who does it have to do with?"

Alex smiled grimly. "Me. Her name is Julia Zarrelli, and my father had her family killed several years ago. She is now seeking her revenge. The beginning of it, at least."

Alex stood up and moved around to her desk. She glanced at the new equipment that had been placed there, knowing that she would be using it to watch the woman very closely. She looked at the empty office on the screen and sighed. "I will not allow her to win this perverted little game of hers. I intend to be ahead of her the whole way." She focused intense blue eyes on Peter and asked sharply, "Now, can you go down there and pretend you don't know any of this? You need to act completely normal around her. You need to give her orders and act like she is just an employee and not the threat that you know she is. Can you do that?" It was imperative to Alex's plan that he go down there and give Julia some non-vital duties to keep her busy. Peter was also to train Patty as far away from the viper as he could and still be in the same building. She wanted to keep her little one as far away from the spider as she could while she spun her web because she intended to be a nice big can of Raid.

Peter was nodding his head. "Yes, I think I can do that. What do you want me to do?"

Alex smiled wickedly and went over her plan step by step with her trusted employee and friend.

*****

There was a knock on Alex's outer door just as she was escorting Peter out of her office. She opened the door and encountered an irate uncle. "Where the hell is Tommy? You have no protection, Alexa!"

Alex shook her head and smiled slightly. The thought of Tommy protecting her made her want to laugh outright, and she had to bite her cheeks. "With Patty. Calm down, Vito, I can take care of myself." She gently propelled Peter toward her door saying, "Peter, you go down to Accounting and send Tommy up after you give the bitch her orders. And Peter, never leave Patty alone. If you have to leave her, call Tommy, wait for him, and then leave. Don't leave her for a minute, even if she insists on it; and believe me, she will insist on it. You will follow my instructions and wait for Tommy or my Uncle Vito. You got that, old friend?"

Peter nodded. "I understand, and don't worry, Alex, I won't leave her alone." His eyes betrayed his fear, but he wasn't afraid for himself, he was afraid for the others.

"Peter, it will be okay. I mean it. I promise you."

"I know, Alex."

She nodded and made a shooing motion. "Okay, off with you, she's waiting." He reluctantly left to go to his office and then the training room.

"Come on, Vito, we've got a lot to discuss," said Alex as she escorted the worried man into her inner sanctum.

*****

Patty was concentrating on a column of numbers. Peter was next to her, smiling and shaking his head in wonder. *The kid really picks things up very quickly. Alex is damn lucky. Patty really is an amazing girl,* he thought affectionately, with a large smile on his face.

Unseen by the two busy occupants, two figures entered the

office. As soon as they saw Patty and Peter, huge grins appeared on their faces. Peter tensed up and looked to see who entered, then suddenly relaxed when he saw who they were.

"Okay, Patty, its break time."

"No, Peter, I've almost got it, " Patty protested, still staring at the numbers floating in front of her on the screen, totally unaware of the presence of the other occupants in the room.

"You will get it, little one. Now all good little worker bees must take their breaks when the queen bee says so. And I do say so, so it is the law," said Alex in an amused voice.

Patty's head jerked up, then her smile matched the one on the face of the dark woman across from her. "Oh, hi!"

"Hi, yourself," replied Alex, her eyes staring into the beautiful green. Patty was so focused on the other woman, she didn't even notice the older man who coughed discreetly.

Alex chuckled and said, "Sorry, Unc."

She crossed the room and put her arm around Patty's shoulders, then turned toward her uncle glowing with pride. "Uncle Vito, this is Patty Darcy. Patty, this is the only truly loving relative I have had since my mother died, my beloved Uncle Vito." Tears were evident in everyone's eyes as these two important people in Alex's life smiled shyly and said quiet hellos to each other.

Discreetly, Peter left the room to the family that was forming right before his eyes. He felt pretty choked up himself and very happy for his old friend. Vito walked over to Patty, put a gentle thumb under her chin and said, "So you're the little girl who stole my darling's heart?"

Patty met the kind eyes that were looking deeply into hers, and then replied shyly, "Yes, sir, I guess I am. And you're the man who made it possible for her to love me. Thank you so much, sir..."

"Please call me, Uncle Vito."

"It would be an honor, Uncle Vito."

Alex stood back, leaning against a wall just watching the two most important people in her life acknowledge each other.

Tears fell from her eyes as she watched them hug each other. She walked over and hugged them both. Looking into two sets of equally teary eyes, she cleared her throat and said, "Can I interest anyone in an early lunch?"

*****

Julia Zarrelli entered her domain, putting her purse in a drawer, turning on the computer—all the normal things a secretary would do at the beginning of her day. At Toys, she was known as Julie Rani. She was pleased that she had accomplished the first step of her plan—she'd made Alex Bennett notice a deadly presence in her company. And, she was positive that no one would suspect her of Robby's murder. She was expert at hiding behind her innocent façade. She was also an expert at hiding her emotions, She and her Uncle Tomas had been the sole survivors of the Bennett Vendetta and now, thanks to her intellect and cunning, they were both well placed under cover in her enemy's company. She knew that soon they would be able to taste the sweetness of the revenge that they were after.

What Julia hadn't expected was how hands-on the dark woman was at Toys. She'd thought Alex was just a figurehead, and all her energy was centered on Murder Inc. However, Alex was deeply involved in all aspects of Toys Inc., and left most of Murder Inc. to her Uncle Vito. This was a complete surprise to the redhead. Alex was everywhere in Toys, with her fingers in every pie, but Julia wasn't worried, She knew she could bide her time and act like a total innocent around the powerful woman. After all, why should Alex suspect a humble innocent like her of being capable killing one of her deadly operatives? She smiled wickedly as she began to go through her emails and correspondence for her busy boss.

Robby was easy to take out; in fact, he was like a stupid fish in a barrel, she thought to herself with a smirk as she sorted through the letters. *Now I have to get Alex's little girl friend. That new girl is more then just a casual friend to the dark woman. Miss High and Mighty Bennett is in love with that innocent; and if I take her out, the bitch would be crippled.* Her eyes became slightly crazed, so she leaned back in her chair and closed them so that no one would be able to read in them how she felt. She took a deep breath, clearing her mind of all thought; and when she opened her eyes, they no longer betrayed her emotions.

*****

Patty was safely in accounting with Tommy and Peter. Vito was comfortably seated in Alex's chair, and Alex was sitting on a corner of her desk with arms crossed, watching their quarry on the new surveillance equipment.

"Well, she certainly is acting legit, huh?"

"Yeah, well I didn't expect to see her draw out maps and timetables planning my demise, Unc. I really think that she has more brains than that," replied Alex with a chuckle, shaking her head.

"Then what the hell do you expect to see, Alexa?"

"I haven't the slightest idea. I just know I need to keep an eye on her…Wait, Unc, who the hell is that?"

*****

"What the hell are you doing here?" Julia asked her uncle who had just snuck into her office and was leaning against a file cabinet with a cruel smirk on his face.

"Relax, Julia. No one is here right now. Where is your boss, anyway?"

"Upstairs, training the big boss' new protégé. "

A huge, cruel smile spread across his large face. "Ah, our sweet little target, huh? So are we finally going to make our move?"

A matching smile lit up Julia's face. "Very soon. The bitch

is more involved on this side than I suspected. She is always around this part of the office. In order for the plan to work, I need to get the little innocent alone; so, I have to make sure that the terror of the world isn't around. What the hell are you doing here, Uncle?" She looked over his shoulder to make sure no one was overhearing them, walked over and closed the door, then turned back toward the older man.

"I just thought I could help you when you take the girlfriend hostage."

"No, I don't need you then. If I can't take care of one little innocent, I am not the daughter of Franco Zarrelli."

*****

Alex was pacing in front of the monitor, and she was seething. Her eyes were pure ice, and danger radiated from every pore as her enemy casually discussed harming her beloved. Alex looked like a panther about to pounce.

"Uncle Vito, we need to get Patty out of here. Right now! I'll take her home, with Tommy to protect her. I trust him, and no else will get near her. My God, she just casually threatened the sweetest human being on this planet like she was ordering lunch…We need to move…"

"Wait, Alexa they're still plotting. Listen…"

*****

"I found the safe house, so now I can take the other one out…"

"No, not just yet. First we take out the innocent, because she means everything to Bennett. The assassin is just icing on the cake. After we kill her sweet little girlfriend, then we'll go after her operative. Then, we take out the uncle. That way we'll destroy her bit by bit. Then it will just be a showdown between the bitch and me; and I will obliterate her…"

Ri

*****

"Oh, we will have a showdown, my evil friend; but it will be at a time and place of my choosing," Alex promised the woman on the screen in a quiet dangerous voice. "Come on, Vito, I want to get Patty to safety right now. I don't like being a sitting duck!"

Chapter Eight
Private Retreat

"Okay, wrap it up, you three," said Alex, smiling in the office doorway. Three pairs of surprised eyes looked over to the tall, dark haired executive.

"Change in venue. Patty and Tommy are coming home with me, and Peter, there is a new assignment for you. Go to my office please, and it will all be explained," she said calmly, knowing that Vito was waiting there for Peter to relay her instructions. Peter nodded and quietly left the Accounting office.

"Okay, you two, come on, we don't have all day, you know," she said.

"Alex...?"

"When we get in the car, love. Just get your stuff together, and let's go," said Alex quietly, as she gently led the women she loved to the door.

Tommy followed obediently, and the three of them were silent until they were safely in Alex's limo. Once safely inside her very secure limo, she calmly explained the situation to her confused companions.

"Sorry for the mystery. I now know that Patty here is a

definite target, and I had to get you out of there, sweetheart. That bitch Julia calmly said that she was going to hurt you, and I won't let you anywhere near her now. I had to get you to safety as soon as I could, so I'm taking you home, which is the safest place I know."

Patty's eyes widened in surprise. "Why would I be a target?"

Alex enfolded the small woman in her arms. "Somehow the bitch knows that I love you. It's all a part of her damn master plan—you and Uncle Vito—but my uncle can take care of himself. You, my little love, need to be protected. My house is safe; and with Tommy there as extra muscle, I will feel much better. I can't act unless I know you're safe, and I trust Tommy to keep you that way." She looked over Patty's shoulder into her old friend's understanding eyes.

"I'll keep her safe, Boss. What are we going to do?"

Alex sighed, wrapped her arm around Patty's shoulders gently pulling the blonde head against her chest, absently running her fingers through the soft hair. She smiled grimly at Tommy. "First, we get this one to safety." She leaned down, gently kissing Patty's forehead. Patty looked up lovingly at Alex and rubbed her cheek against the tall woman's neck.

Alex hugged her tighter as she continued, "Then, once you have her all safe and sound, I will go and confront the lunatic..."

"No!" Patty said, her body suddenly filling with tension. She pulled back a bit and cried, "Please Alex, I can't lose you..."

"You won't, sweetheart. I must strike out with this knowledge as soon as I can, before she..."

"Yes, but why fire against fire. Why can't you use water and put the fire out?"

"What?"

"Instead of a showdown with you getting shot at, why don't you just set her up to be arrested for Robby's murder? After all, she did kill him. I'm sure you can discreetly let the police in on it..."

"Hmmm, I never even thought of that. Patty, you are a wonder! I was so blinded by my anger, that I didn't even consider the obvious." She kissed the younger woman passionately and then rubbed noses with her playfully. "You are brilliant. Did you know that?"

Patty's eyes were bright with tears. "No, I'm not. I just don't want to lose you. I'm desperate…"

"So am I, my love. You're seeing things that I can't. Thank you, my darling." Alex kissed her passionately again. Tommy was very uncomfortable so he stared out the window, suddenly interested in the sight of the busy traffic. *Wish I sat up front with the driver; Its getting awfully hot back here,* thought Tommy as he watched the cars whiz by.

Alex looked over Patty's shoulder and smiled apologetically at her old friend. "Oops. Sorry, Tommy. I forgot that you were there."

"S'kay, Boss. Now, what do we do?"

"Same idea, just a little different twist. We go to my house and try to figure out how to point the police in the right direction. Meanwhile, we keep this one safe." Alex pulled Patty onto her lap, holding her against her body in a protective embrace.

*****

When Peter entered Alex's office, he found Vito waiting patiently for him.

"Sit down, Peter," Vito instructed the young man quietly.

Peter crossed to the visitor's chair that he had occupied earlier in the day. He sat down quietly and looked up expectantly at the older man. To Peter, this was a rather shady figure. Vito was around Toys once in a while, but mostly stayed in Las Vegas. When he was here, he said very little to the employees of Toys.

"It's not your fault, but the woman you hired wants to take out me and little Patty. We ain't going to let that happen. Alex is taking care of Patty and I can take care of me, but we still need your help, Peter. Are you willing?"

"Is it legal?"

Vito smiled and said softly, "Of course it is. It's not my plan, it's Alexa's; and she wouldn't ask you to do anything illegal. Don't you know that by now?"

Peter nodded his head.

"Good, this is what we need you to do…"

*****

They arrived at the house and were met by the butler and Alex's head of security. Tommy quickly escorted Patty inside the house, while Alex listened to the precautions they had already taken. She detailed her orders for them to strengthen the ring of security around her home. Once satisfied with the arrangements, she followed Tommy and Patty inside, where she found them waiting for her in the foyer. Alex politely asked Tommy to make himself comfortable in her den, then she took Patty's small hand, led her upstairs to their bedroom and hugged the blonde tightly.

Patty returned the warm hug, resting her head on Alex's shoulder as she asked the taller woman, "Are we really safe here?

Alex gently kissed her forehead. "Yes, I'm making sure that there are both physical and electronic sweeps of the area every ten minutes…"

"But won't that be expensive?" Patty protested.

"I don't care whether it is or not; I will not allow that woman anywhere near you. You are my life. I couldn't care less about money when your life is at stake." She hugged her fiercely once again. Then she picked the smaller woman up and carried her to their large bed. Alex started to undress Patty, slowly kissing every area as it was exposed.

"I think we'll be in conference for the rest of the day," Alex whispered hoarsely as she nibbled a pink ear.

Patty could barely breathe, let alone respond. She did the only thing she could. She gently pulled back and met the lips of the woman she loved in a passionate kiss. When they parted, she whispered, "Alex, I know you love me and want to protect me. I just wish I could ease your burden."

Alex caressed her soft cheek and replied softly, "But you already are...Please believe that. Damn, you are so beautiful." She kissed her passionately again, then began to caress every inch of available skin until they both fell over the edge, forgetting their problems in the pure bliss of the moment.

*****

"Alex, what are we going to do?" Patty asked as they cuddled in the large, antique bed.

"We're going to implement your plan," Alex replied between kisses on the sweet neck beneath her.

Enjoying the attention, Patty tilted her head, exposing more neck. "How?"

"I have many talents," purred the dark woman as she continued her descent down toward Patty's beautiful breasts.

"I already know that very well," replied the panting blonde as her hands caressed Alex's strong back. "But what are we going to do?"

Alex was teasing Patty's breast with her tongue and she looked up with passionate eyes. "Do we really have to discuss this right now?"

"Yes, because I can't relax until...I...um...have some idea...of your plans..." She paused as she wriggled under her love's aggressive assault on her now erect breasts.

Alex stopped the ministrations and gently kissed the valley between Patty's hot mounds, as she looked into the passionate green eyes with a smirk. Moving up until she was next to the small blonde, she held her in a warm embrace, kissed her gently, and then pulled back so she could look into her eyes as she replied. "All right, let's discuss this quickly, because I think we both need to get back to the issue at hand." Patty giggled, and Alex smiled at her love's merriment. "You remember Jaust, my friend on the police force, from when Robby screwed up at the mall." Patty nodded, then looked down. Alex gently lifted her chin and looked intently into the loving green eyes. "That was the luckiest day of my life because I met and fell in love with you, all with in a few minutes," she said with a beaming smile.

Patty smiled back and nodded. "Mine, too."

They kissed tenderly, then Alex pulled back, determined to get this over with so she could truly make love to the woman in her arms. "Well, Tommy is calling him right now to advise him of the little fiend's plans and her involvement with Robby's death. In addition to the police investigation, Peter is giving her a major job to keep her and her uncle busy. Hopefully, when she finds out about the police investigating her, that it will put her off balance so much that it will disrupt all her rotten plots against us. Does that satisfy you, my love?" She said all that in one breath. She was anxious to get back to the matter at hand, which was loving Patty.

Patty nodded and kissed the dark woman. Her breasts, erect with need, rubbed against Alex's already excited body. "Yes."

"Good. Now lets get back to what's really important, you." Alex continued down the path she had begun earlier, knowing that it would lead them to temporarily forget their problems as they enjoyed their deep bond.

*****

Alex was in her office on the second floor of her mansion, pacing in front of an uncomfortable Tommy. She was trying to figure out how to use him to safely get Val out of the safe house. The dilemma was that she wanted to go take care of it herself, and yet she couldn't bring herself to leave Patty for a minute. She trusted Tommy and her staff, but she needed to protect Patty herself.

"We'll just have to let Vito do what he wants and go extract her," said Tommy quietly to his distraught boss.

"Under normal circumstances, that's exactly what I'd do. These aren't normal circumstances, damn it! Vito is a target too, remember? I can't ask him to risk his life…"

"Vito can take care of himself, Boss. He wouldn't want you to risk Patty for him, and you know it," Tommy argued reasonably.

Alex nodded her head in acknowledgment. "You're right about that. Shit. This is such a mess! What the hell are we going to do?" She finally settled in her comfortable chair, crossing her arms and leaning her head back against the headrest, exhausted.

"We are going to get Val out and keep Patty safe."

"Gee, that's brilliant. How?"

"I'll get Val out and take her to the new safe house, and you stay here with Patty. Simple, huh?"

Alex shook her head with a grim expression. "Simplistic, you mean. The bitch probably has the safe house staked out. If you move Val out, she will kill her, and probably you, too. No. The only way to do this is to figure a way to move Val without it seeming like it's happening."

"How?"

"I don't know! If I did, we wouldn't be having this conversation; I'd be god damned doing it!" Alex exploded, getting up and pacing like a caged panther again.

There was a soft knock on the door, and a blonde head popped in. Tommy was astounded by his boss's sudden change of expression. She went from scowling anger to bright joy in the blink of an eye.

"Hello, love. What's wrong?" Alex asked Patty gently.

"That's exactly what I was going to ask you. I thought I heard shouting," said Patty quietly, a sweet smile on her face.

Through her bangs, Alex looked at Patty sheepishly. " Um, I…uh was…I'm sorry."

"Why were you shouting, sweetheart?"

Alex went to her love; needing to feel her close, she enfolded her in her arms, hugging her tightly. Then she brought her head back slightly so she could see the concerned green eyes, "I'm just trying to work out some logistics, and I got a little frustrated."

Patty gently brushed some hair back out of the beautiful blue eyes and asked, "Am I the reason for the frustration?"

Alex nodded and looked down, unable to meet those very honest green eyes. Patty wouldn't allow her to do that. She guided her head back up by gently lifting her chin with a soft index finger. Their eyes met, and Patty said, "Please tell me what's happening. Maybe I can actually help."

Tommy decided to speak up, even though it might provoke Alex's famous temper. "Why not, Alex? We're going in circles by ourselves."

Alex turned toward her trusted friend and briskly nodded her head. "Okay, it can't hurt."

She led Patty to the couch, sitting down and patting the seat next to her. After Patty sat down, Alex patted her chest and smiled in invitation. Smiling back, Patty lay back against Alex's warm chest. Alex affectionately encircled her love in her arms, and explained their problem.

"Valerie's position has been compromised, and we have to find a way to get her out without telegraphing it to Zarrelli. I'm split in two on this, my darling. I know I should go to the site and remove Val, but I can't leave you. I know logically that you are very well protected here, and I do trust everyone, but emotionally, I can't leave you. I'm sorry..I…"

Though she had no idea why, Alex felt tears slowly form in her eyes. Patty gently dried the tears with her fingers.

Patty was touched on so many levels by what she was witnessing. First, the trust that Alex placed in her by sharing her plans and being open about her distress at not knowing what to do. Also, that Alex was crying because she loved her and didn't want to leave her.

The most touching to Patty was that Alex was apologizing

for being unsure of her emotions. This strong woman was being so very open with her and allowing her to see her true heart. All this, despite the fact that it might cause her to look weak in front of her subordinate. Tommy was touched too, and flashed a smile at Patty when she met his eyes.

"There's no need to be sorry, sweetheart. I know this is all pure love. I think you should determine the logistics and go get Val. I'm well protected here, right, Tommy?"

"That's what I said, kiddo. The Boss is still worried about you, and I can't blame her, "Tommy replied he was touched by the sweet scene unfolding before him.

Alex looked back and forth between her love and her friend, and shook her head. She couldn't argue against the logic. She couldn't fight her instincts, either; and they were screaming for her to stay with Patty. When things went down, she would be needed. She trusted them completely, so she looked into two sets of concerned eyes, cleared her throat and said quietly, "I know that you're both right. Logically, it all makes sense…but I can't be logical. My instincts say that I'm going to be needed, and I can't leave you alone. I can't!" she cried. The arms around Patty tightened, and Alex laid her head possessively on Patty's shoulder.

Patty gently stroked the soft dark hair. "Okay, then, we execute plan B. Tommy and Vito go and help Val, but you plan the strategy."

Alex's head popped up, surprised blue eyes meeting the serious green eyes. Nodding her head, she agreed. "Yes…yes, that's right! If I plan it really carefully, Tommy and Vito should be able to go in and get Val out, and no one will get hurt. Patty, you're so damned brilliant!!" She began to kiss the smaller woman's neck.

"I think I'll go get some coffee while you two confer," muttered Tommy, getting out while the getting was good. He had just cleared the door and was closing it as a burst of giggles broke out on the other side of the room.

*****

Peter walked briskly into his office, where he came face to face with his secretary. He had his orders and he would follow them to the letter, trusting that his boss knew what she was doing.

"Miss Rani, I have an important project for you. Please come into my office."

Julia looked up from her desk, nodded, and meekly followed the older man into his office. She sat demurely, and looking up at him with innocent eyes.

Damn, she is good, thought Peter as he watched her play her part.

"Per the CEO's instructions, I'm going to redesign our logging system, and I want to assign the project to you. I need you and one of our engineers to initiate the project, and the first stage is due next Friday. I will give you all the graphics you need so you and the engineer that Miss Bennett assigns can set up the system. I really need you to put in your total effort in on this, since Miss Bennett want the first stage completed as soon as possible. I know that you're new, and so I need to know if you have any personal issues that will prevent you from completing this project on schedule."

Julia was stunned. It was an important project, and she could see that it was an excellent opportunity. To keep her current position, she couldn't turn it down. On the other hand, this was going to throw a wrench in her plans. She decided to go with the flow and see if it opened an opportunity for her to strike at the enemy.

"No, sir, I have no problems with my time."

Peter nodded and sat down behind his desk, "Very well. Do you have your pad?" She held it up. "Good. Let's start with the new matrix of the system."

*****

Knowing Peter would follow instructions to the letter, Vito headed to Alex's place to find out the next step in her plan. He knew Alex had confidence in him, he just didn't have any in himself. His brother had made sure that he always knew just how inept he was; that his young niece was far better able to handle the business at 18 years of age than he had when he was in his late 30's.

That feeling still stayed in his heart, and he had always seen Alex as a superior intellect. It never diminished the love and affection he felt for her, but it annoyed the hell out of the dark woman.

He arrived at the mansion and headed right for the security office to make sure they were following all the precautions that he and Alex had discussed earlier. Satisfied that all was well, he went into the house and headed straight for the stairs so he could talk to Alex in her office.

"Uh, I wouldn't disturb Alex right now, sir," Tommy said quietly from the living room door. He'd heard the older man as he entered the house, and thought it would be better to head him off before he got embarrassed.

"Why the hell not?"

"Um…she and Patty are in conference."

"Conference? What are…Oh…Oh, I see what you mean."

Tommy smiled at the older man, who smiled back knowingly.

"So, what are you doing to kill the time?"

"Watching TV and waiting for the all clear signal."

"Would you mind some company?"

"Of course not. Do you like football?"

"You bet your ass I do, kid."

*****

Alex and Patty were still cuddling on the couch in Alex's office.

"Do you think Peter has begun your plan?"

"Yes, Peter is damned loyal. He would have made sure that the bitch is overwhelmingly busy, and this project utilizes her scumbag of an uncle, too. I hope it at least keeps them off balance."

"It will. You are so brilliant."

"It takes one to know one," Alex replied as she licked her love playfully on the nose. She tenderly kissed each eye and brushed the hair back from them.

"You melt my heart. Did you know that? All I have to do is look at you, and my heart melts. You just fill me up with such happiness. Please believe me when I tell you that 'happiness' is an inept word to describe how I feel, my love. Thank you for coming into my life; you made me a better person. I love you with all my heart."

Tears were falling from her eyes, and Patty threw her arms around the dark woman's neck, hugging her tightly to her.

"I love you so much; I can't believe you feel the same. You are so very special. I'm overwhelmed by these feelings—you make me feel so strong and happy. Thank you so much."

Alex kissed Patty passionately, then seductively moved down the soft neck as she whispered against it, "All I want from you is pure love. I really don't need or want any thanks. I'm the one full of gratitude."

There was a knock on the door, and Alex's head popped up, her expression changed suddenly to pure annoyance. "What!?!"

Patty stroked her hair and cooed to her, trying to keep her calm as the butler said through the door, "Madam, Mr. Bennett was wondering when you would be coming downstairs?"

Alex looked at Patty and rolled her eyes. "Tell him, in about an hour…"

"Alex," Patty whispered, "he's concerned about Val."

Alex caressed her cheek and whispered, "Priorities?"

Patty leaned into the caress and smiled as she whispered back, "We have been up here a long time."

Alex snorted and hugged the other woman to her, "Well,

this is far more important to me then anything else; but you are right, of course, my love. Val's life does come first. Um, we will continue this later, right?"

"Yes, please," Patty replied, hugging Alex tightly against her.

Alex lifted her head and met the soft lips in a tender kiss. Then she pulled back and rubbed noses with her saying, "Deal."

Hand in hand, Alex and Patty walked into Alex's den, amused to find the men in the room completely immersed in watching a football game on the large screen TV. Alex rolled her eyes as she bent down to whisper, "I think we could have stayed upstairs for a while, don't you?"

Patty smiled up at her and nodded. Alex winked back, then cleared her throat as loudly as she could.

"Excuse me, gentlemen, I believe you requested our presence."

Vito jumped up from the large comfortable chair in which he had been sitting. "Alexa! About goddamn time! Have you decided what to do about Val?"

Alex shook her head as she smiled grimly. She strode over to the coffee table and used the remote to turn off the TV, "I see you boys have been in a deep conference over this issue."

"That's not fair, boss. You're the strategist; we were waiting for you," said Tommy, his voice betraying how hurt he was that his boss and friend would think he would be playing instead of taking action when Val's life was at stake.

"That may be true, but you both have very good brains. I would like this to be an exchange of ideas, not just me spouting orders. Vito, Tommy, I am not an all-knowing goddess. I don't have all the answers. I...I'm..." She began to falter, then felt the warm hand gently stroking her back. She looked down and smiled, locking eyes with Patty and gaining strength through the contact. Alex took a deep breath and continued. "Come on, boys, let's have a real meeting."

The two men nodded in agreement. As the four sat down

for an interactive discussion of tactics, Alex really hoped that this was how all her meetings would be conducted from then on.

*****

A familiar truck pulled up in front of the nondescript house in the unremarkable neighborhood. Two men wearing the uniform of the local telephone company hopped out of the truck and walked nonchalantly up to the front door of the small house.

The older man was holding a clipboard, and the younger one was carrying a toolbox. The rhythmic knock on the front door was one Val recognized as the safe signal that Alex had devised. She answered the door cautiously and was surprised by the sight that greeted her. Val invited the men in, ostensibly to do their jobs. Tommy shook his head, saying that he was going to check the lines out back. Vito followed Val into the house.

"What the hell is going on?"

Vito responded to her concern in a quiet professional voice. "The bitch knows where you are, and we're getting you out and moving you right under their stupid noses. Tommy is moving the truck out back into the alley, and I'm going to slip out to another safe place that Alex has secured.

"How…?"

"I don't know; damn it, Val! Do you want to take anything with you other than that?" he asked, pointing to the pearl-handled revolver in her hand.

"No, I'm ready to go."

"Okay, kid. Move, now!"

*****

Alex was driving her convertible up the mountain road as fast as seemed safe. She kept checking her side mirrors to make sure they hadn't picked up a tail.

"Alex, we are going to get the police on our tail if you don't slow down."

Alex smiled and decelerated. It had been decided at their strategy meeting that Alex and Patty would go up to Alex's private retreat. Both Vito and Alex felt that location would be far safer then her mansion. And that was why she found herself speeding up the mountain—to get them up there before dark. Not a living soul except Vito knew where her hideaway was, because Alex had never invited anyone to it. She regretted the reason that she had to take her little one up to her favorite place, but she was very happy to finally have someone special to share it with, the woman she loved.

"It's another hour at this snail's pace. Are you sure you want me to go this slowly?"

"Yes, my darling. I think it would be better if we arrived in one piece to see this wonderland of yours, don't you?"

Alex chuckled and reached over to cares Patty's cheek. "Not quite wonderland, my love, it's a bit too rustic. I think…um, I hope you like it."

"I'm sure I will. I can't wait to see it, Alex, really!" She noticed an eyebrow rising in question. "No, Alex, please, let's go at a snail's pace."

Alex nodded and kept the speed at a mere 80 miles per hour instead of the 120 that the Mazarati was capable of. Besides, she couldn't be touching her love if she drove too fast, and Alex was enjoying the feel of the soft skin as they drove to the cabin.

*****

After depositing an argumentative and testy Val at the new safe house, Tommy and Vito headed back to the office per Alex's instructions. They were both pleased and surprised at how smoothly the whole operation had gone. They had slipped Val out of the house through a grove of trees in the back yard,

Rᵢ

out a gate, to the alley where the truck was waiting. Tommy and Val pulled out in the van, while Vito went back out through the front door of the house, making a show of talking to the already departed resident. The truck was waiting out front to pick him up. Without any fuss, they drove at the legal speed to Val's new safe house location.

Now they were about a mile from the office, and Vito was mentally reviewing the meeting he'd had with his niece. Vito was astonished at Alex's feelings that a group discussion was better than making all the final plans herself. She had such a brilliant mind that it never occurred to him that when it came to such an important decision, she would want to consider the thoughts of others.

He could tell Tommy was not fazed by any of it. After they'd left the mansion to get the truck, the younger man had told him that this had been coming for a long time. He told Vito that this was her style of management at Toys, and as far as he could see, every day she had been transforming into a typical executive. The seething, angry gun-for-hire was long gone.

"I just don't think you realize how much she loves Toys and hates MI. This transition has been happening for years, Vito. Patty was just the catalyst that made it complete, but she was changing long before they fell in love. She is simply not that angry, uncontrollable girl who took over the family."

Remembering that Alex, they were both silent as they drove toward the safe house. She had truly been mad with grief when her father was killed when she was 18 years old. The entire year following her father's murder, it was the blood lust that had been her driving force. During that time, in a fit of rage, she had almost stabbed Vito to death . The realization that she had almost killed the only living person who still loved her had finally snapped her out of her murderous haze.

Vito had calmly ensured that she was back on an even keel. She still ran the family with an iron fist, but Vito made sure she went back to school and got her masters degree in engineering and computer science. It was during her final year that she had started Toys as a phony front for Murder, Inc., but as she became involved with developing her brainchild, she fell in love with Toys, Inc. She loved being a legitimate businesswoman, and found she was very good at it; and she began to despise every aspect of the family business. She slowly transferred major parts of MI to Las Vegas, and her uncle, and away from her.

Until one day, while Christmas shopping at the mall, a mistake brought her face to face with her future, and she never looked back. Tommy and Vito smiled at each other, both hoping that this dream would come true for Alex. She deserved that future.

*****

The future was twirling in the foyer of Alex's cabin in pure joy at the beauty of it. Fondly, Alex watched her beloved spinning in circles, a smile of love on her face and reflected in her glowing blue eyes.

"So, I take it that this means you like it, huh?" she asked the smaller woman with a lopsided grin.

Patty stopped, and after balancing herself to control her dizzy head, she looked up at Alex in astonishment.

"Of course...Oh." She stopped mid sentence when she realized she was being tweaked. She laughed and hit the older woman on the arm. "Oh you," she scolded as she entered the cabin.

Alex chuckled as she bent down to pick up their bags, following the sweetest woman she has ever known into their private nest.

*****

Tommy sat at his desk, working intently on his computer as the assistant chief engineer entered his office. He never

105

glanced up or even acknowledged the older man, he just gestured toward the chairs and kept working. He could barely keep himself from growling at the older Zarrelli for putting his boss and her beloved in danger. But, Alex had a plan of action; and he would follow it, no matter how much he wanted to forget it and just beat the crap out of the perpetrator.

"Sit down...please," he said, trying to remember to be civil, at least. Under the circumstances, his usual friendly persona was absent.

The big man sat down and fidgeted. He was very uncomfortable with being summoned to the CEO's office. He felt the jig was up and was trying to figure the best way to escape when the buzzer on Tommy's desk went off.

Tommy looked up and said briskly, "Go on in," then immediately went back to his keyboard.

The engineer nervously entered the elegant office. His face reflected surprise when he was met, not by the raven-haired beauty, but by her uncle instead. Vito was sitting behind the large desk and looked up with a look of calm command.

"Sit," said Vito in a professional manner. In reality, all he wanted to do was to take this man's head, twist it off, and toss it like a basketball out the penthouse window. Alexa had a plan of attack, and he would not jeopardize that with his anger. Despite his revulsion at the sight of his enemy, he smiled cordially and acted according to business etiquette.

Zarrelli fidgeted in the big comfortable visitor's chair. He now really felt trapped, and was trying to figure how to get out of the situation. Vito smiled inwardly. *Yes, slime, you are caught; but my Alexa is not ready to spring the trap...yet. For what you did to Robby and are threatening to do Patty and me, she wants our friend Jaust to put his nice shiny bracelets on your wrists.* Vito just hoped they would be caught quickly; he knew that this was making his niece and her love very nervous, and it wasn't doing much good for his condition either..

"Miss Bennett would like to use your talents for a new project. You will be working with a Miss Rani in our sales department, putting together a new logging system for the internal computer network. Miss Bennett wants it completed by this Friday. Do you think you could handle that?"

The look of astonishment on the man's face made Vito wish they had some of the surveillance equipment in Alex's office so she could see it.

"You...a...mean you..."

"Well, if you feel you can't..."

"Oh, no sir, I can do it. I was just so surprised. I do want to do it, though."

Vito nodded. "Okay, then. Go to it, man. Miss Rani will advise you on what's needed."

Vito watched him sprint out of the office and said quietly after the door closed, "The trap is set, Alexa."

*****

Alex had her arms around Patty, cuddling on the couch in front of a roaring fire. Though they wore nothing, they still felt like they had no need for the fire. They were quite warm and comfortable. They had just made love, and were simply enjoying the contentment that followed. Alex nibbled Patty's ear, and Patty was tracing the muscles of Alex's taut stomach. Alex licked the rim of the small ear, and grinned seductively as she heard the smaller woman moan in reaction.

Alex pulled back slightly and purred into the ear, "I love it when you make that sound."

Patty leaned into the embrace replying, "Is that why you bring it out all the time?" She tickled the stomach, causing the tall woman to chuckle and hold her even tighter.

"You betcha." She started to kiss along the neckline and said, "You taste so good, I could just hold you like this forever."

"Mmm, that's a perfect time frame for me. I love you so much, Alex...don't...Alex, please don't leave me." She suddenly started to cry, remembering what was happening outside of the cabin.

Alex gently repositioned her so they were facing each other as she wiped the tears from around pretty green eyes. "I will never leave you. I will always be with you. Always. I love you so much, I don't ever want to let you go."

Alex suddenly felt a wave of emotion herself and had to swallow hard to handle the lump of it that was lodged in her throat. She kissed Patty's forehead, and then gently brought the fair head down to rest on her breast.

Patty's heartbeat slowed the moment her head touched Alex's warm skin, and her rhythm became the same as that of the one who was nurturing her. Patty closed her eyes.

"Thank you. I think I needed to hear that right now."

"I mean it, Patty, I don't care what I have to do. I will be with you 'til the day after forever. When we go, it will be when we're old and gray and surrounded by loved ones."

Patty smiled and kissed Alex. "I love you."

"I love you, too, with all my heart and soul," said Alex stroking the long blonde hair. She smiled as she heard the slow breathing and gentle snoring of her love. She kissed the top of her head and said softly, "No matter what the fates have planned, I will never leave you. I promise."

*****

Patty woke up in the same position—cradled in Alex's protective arms, her head comfortably resting on her love's chest. She opened her eyes to find that Alex was still fast asleep, wisps of hair falling over her face. Patty gently brushed the dark hair out of the way so she could see the features more clearly. Big blue eyes fluttered open, and Alex smiled down at her.

"Hi," Patty said softly.

"Hi," replied Alex, gently caressing Patty's cheek.

Patty looked down. "I'm sorry I got so…"

"Shh, it's okay. I feel the same way about you. I know I…I couldn't survive if anything happened to you."

"Don't say that!"

"But it's true. I …would simply die without you. If you were taken, I…I wouldn't…" Now Alex quietly cried at the thought of losing her love.

Patty hugged her tighter and said softly, "Well, we will just have to make sure that it doesn't happen. We need each other too much."

Teary blue eyes met red rimmed green as Alex replied, "Deal, That's a deal."

*****

"So, would you like to learn to fish today, or are you having too much fun changing clothes?" asked Alex, amused, as she watched Patty change into her fourth outfit in a row.

"I want to learn to fish but, Alex, what's appropriate to wear?"

Alex laughed and shook her head, "Sweetheart, any of the clothes you've put on would be fine. I just love watching you change, so go on and play…"

She ducked as a pillow flew at her head. "Good shot," laughing even harder when she saw the pink, frustrated face. She walked over and lifted the small, defiant chin, and smiled into the blushing face as she said very quietly, "I love it when you blush like that." She then kissed the pouting lips. Small arms encircled her waist and returned the kiss with equal passion.

When they parted, Alex chucked her chin and asked, "Better?"

Patty smiled and blushed a bit more replying, "Yes, thank you."

"Would you like me to teach you how to fish now?" Alex asked, as she rubbed noses with the small woman.

"I'd love it."

"Good. Come on, let's go, before all the fish go home.

Two lures bobbed on the placid lake as two happy women rested under the shade of a big oak tree.

"Alex?"

"Mmm?" Alex murmured lazily.

Patty smile widened. She had never seen Alex so relaxed before; it suited the dark woman. Patty wished she could stay that way all the time. "I'm really enjoying this."

Blue eyes popped open, and Alex smiled happily. "Yep, I do, too. When this mess is all over, I'm taking you on a nice long extended vacation. Just you and me, no worries or intrusions. Some place nice and peaceful, like this."

"Wow! Really?"

Alex chuckled at the excited expression on her love's face. "Yeah really."

"I'd really love that."

Suddenly, one of the poles started to bob up and down.

"Patty, your line!" Alex called out, as she jumped up and ran for the bouncing pole. Laughing, they pulled in a big, beautiful fish. Alex's face showed how much she loved the fun and simple relaxation of just fishing. She started to get the fish ready for transport, as she removed the hook; she burst out in a fit of giggles at Patty's squeamish face.

"I suppose this means I will have to skin all your fish, too, huh?" asked Alex with a glowing expression on her face.

"Ewww! Oh, Alex, do I have to skin it?"

Alex shook her head and smirking said, "Its okay, love; I'll do it. I'm very used to it. I did it all the time as a kid."

"Really? Did your Uncle Vito teach you?"

Alex nodded her head.

"Yeah. He used to take me out to a fishing hole on weekends. And then someplace different every school break. It was the only time I felt...well, normal, I guess. I mean, I was just a kid, not the Godfather's kid."

The dark head was bent as she carefully dropped the fish

into a bucket. She spoke quietly with her back towards the smaller woman. "I've missed this, the simplicity." She turned back to Patty and smiled, though there were tears in her eyes.

"I'm glad we came here."

"Thank you for bringing me, love. I'm really enjoying this," said Patty quietly. She had been very moved by Alex's words and her obvious need for peace.

"It was my pleasure," said Alex, looking into the beautiful green eyes through the fringe of her bangs. She stood and picked up an old towel, wiping her hands. Then she held out her hand to help Patty up, saying, "Come on, love. Let's set up the pole for your next prize fish."

Chapter Nine
Disaster

J ulia and Eric were working side by side in her office. Peter had already left for the day, as had most of the staff.

"Well, aren't we lucky I was the engineer that Ms High and Mighty picked?"

Julia's head snapped up, and she thought, *Yeah, lucky. Is this too easy? No. There is no way Peter could know who I am; and Alex hasn't even been in the office all day. Mmm, just fate, I guess.*

"Uncle Eric, I do have an idea. We can do it tonight, after were done with this project of hers."

"Why are we doing this, anyway? I mean, why help that bitch?"

"Just look at it this way, it's the perfect cover for a little sabotage," she said with an insane twinkle in her eyes.

Eric, touched by the same insanity, smiled brightly. "As well as kidnapping, or instead of?"

"Well, Uncle, we can't kidnap her if she isn't here, so we need to be adaptable. I thought a nice explosion here in her pet company might just get her attention."

"Oooh, that is good, kid. That is very good," They smiled at each other as they continued to work and plan.

*****

Peter entered his outer office, noticing a pile of data on a side credenza. He walked over to check it out and noticed a wire sticking out of the mass of paper. Looking at it with a confused expression, he tugged on the wire. Suddenly there was smoke and loud roar. Then absolute silence.

*****

Vito arrived at Alex's cabin around dinnertime. As he knocked, he could hear music softly playing inside. A cautious dark head peered out the slowly opening door. Blue eyes met Vito's and visibly relaxed. She pulled the snub-nosed revolver back out if its hiding place in her jacket pocket, and slipped it back into the ankle holster where she'd been keeping since the initial threat. Standing up, Alex hugged and kissed her favorite relative, and then escorted him into her home.

Vito's smile widened as he saw how much like a home the cabin had become. Gone was the sterile, barely homey interior. It was full of flowers and Patty's knick-knacks; her cat snuggled comfortably on a pillow by the couch. The stereo was playing soft jazz music, and the smell of home made cooking teased his nose. Patty came in and gave the older man a hug and kiss. "Uncle Vito, it's great to see you. Can you stay for dinner? We have plenty."

"Yes, munchkin, I can stay. From what I smell, your cooking is wonderful."

Alex was smiling broadly as she put one arm around Vito and the other around Patty.

"Well, I didn't even help, so it will be so much better, huh? Sit down, Unc. How long until dinner is ready, love?"

"Oh, about thirty minutes. Um, do you want me to…?

"No, honey, that is not necessary for what I need to tell you. You both will want to know about this."

Instantly alert, Alex's eyebrows shot up and her expression transformed in seconds from that of his relaxed niece to the head of MI.

"What happened, Uncle Vito? Is Val okay? Was she compromised?"

"No, Val is fine. Your extraction plan went perfectly, It's...um please sit down."

Alex and Patty met in the center of the large sofa. Alex enfolded her love in her long, comforting arms. They sat down together and looked up at him.

"Well, what happened then?" Alex asked in a quiet voice, the voice of a commander about to hear that her battle was won, but at some horrible cost.

Vito sat in a large comfortable chair and closed his eyes to gather the strength to tell them what he had to. He opened his eyes to meet concerned blue and frightened green.

"There was an explosion at the office...um...Peter was seriously injured. He is expected to recover, but he may never see..."

Alex jumped out of Patty's arms in a pure rage. She began to pace like an angry tiger.

"Its all my fault! Fuck!" she yelled, shaking the rafters with the strength of her anguished cry. "I shouldn't have left that bitch in my building...I should have....I should..."

Suddenly there were small arms around her waist, stopping her in her tracks. "Stop!" Patty said loudly, so it would break through Alex's rage.

Alex stared at her, stunned into silence by Patty's strong voice and her temerity.

"You can't read other people's minds, Alex. You are not a Goddess. It's just like you said at the meeting this morning— you're a human being, just like Vito and me. You are a very remarkable human being, but you're not all-knowing. Now, please sit down," She gently led the still angry woman to the couch and sat down beside her.

"Am I right or wrong?"

Alex's eyes, which seconds before were blazing with anger, now shone with unshed tears and confusion.

"Yes, you're right. What are we going to do? Vito, you said he'll survive. What condition is he in, exactly? Where is he? How bad are his burns?"

"Shh, Alexa, Come now. I brought you the reports from the hospital. I knew you would need to see them." He pulled them out of his satchel and handed them to his anxious niece.

After reading the report, Alex didn't feel any better, but she was calmer. Peter would live. He had third degree burns on his hands and face. All the burns were treatable, and he would recover fully—except for his eyes. Her brilliant vice president would never see his own software again.

"Oh, God, Patty," She finally allowed the flood of emotions to overtake her, and she cried softly onto Patty's shoulder. Patty gently stroked her hair and held her close, trying to soothe her with her voice as much as she could.

Vito put their dinner in the refrigerator, turned off the music, and kissed them both goodnight. Then he went to sleep in the guestroom.

Patty gently guided Alex to their room and prepared them both for bed. Once they were settled in each other's arms, she began to kiss and talk sweetly into the distraught woman's ear, trying to soothe the pain in any way she could.

Alex's eyes met Patty's and she quietly asked, "How did I ever get so damn lucky to meet you and have you as part of my life? Damn, you are the most remarkable woman. Thank you, darling. I love you."

"I love you, too. I didn't do anything but tell you the truth and love you. That's not remarkable."

"Yes, it is. Patty, no one has ever stopped me in the middle of one of my rages like you just did. You are something else. You are so brave and so damn strong when you need to be." She hugged Patty even closer. "Yet, so soft and adorable. God above, I love you. Patty, if I don't survive…"

"Shh, stop please. Don't say that. You're not going to die. I won't let you. There has got to be a way for you and that woman not to fight this out. That's what she's after, you know. Nothing less than a fight to the death. It doesn't matter if it is yours or hers. It is only necessary that someone should die. No, I won't let her win this. Ever." She looked into beautiful blue eyes full of tears and love. "Between us, my love, we have the brains to defeat her."

Alex kissed Patty deeply and whispered, "Against the two of us, my love, no one on this earth could defeat us."

Chapter Ten
The Attempt

ights and sirens blaring, an ambulance pulled up at the rear entrance of Mercy Hospital. It was midnight, and there was only a skeleton crew on duty that ran out to assist the two men pulling a gurney out of the back of the emergency vehicle. They rushed through the emergency room doors and were met by a staff doctor who ran with them to a private room.

Once the door was closed, one of the male drivers said quietly, "Okay, you two you can come out." The blanket on top was pushed back to reveal a very healthy Alex, and the drapes below were pulled aside to reveal Patty, in equally good health.

Tommy smiled and held out a hand to Patty. "You okay, small stuff?"

Patty nodded. "Yep, that was an interesting experience, but I don't think I want to ride on the bottom next time."

"Awww, you're always on top," teased the tall brunette, stretching and smiling at the redness on her beloved's face and neck.

"Well, you are!" Patty turned a deep red and put her face in her hands, moaning. Alex chuckled then, remembering why they were there, she sobered and turned to the patient man in the white smock.

"Okay, Sam, how far are we from Peter?"

Dr. Samuel Peterson was Alex's personal doctor and a good friend from high school. He was one of the few real friends she'd ever had. They'd never discussed her family or what they did; he'd just always accepted her as she was. For that, she was very grateful.

When they were in college, he'd hoped she was breaking away from all that horror. It was only a year after she had started Toys and had to go to her old friend for a favor that he saw she was still in it up to her neck. Following an assignment that had gone wrong, he'd removed a bullet from her leg. Puzzled, he'd tried to figure out who was the real Alex: his friend, or the violent woman he knew she was in charge at Murder, Inc.

In the last year, he had begun to see a difference. She had been conflicted about MI for years, but in the last year—from the little she'd said—he'd realized she'd had more than enough of that world and wanted to get away from it.

She was slowly trying to pull away from that side of the business and lead the life she was meant to. The real Alex—a basically good person—was emerging, and he felt it was about time.

As he studied her while she was being playful with her friend, he saw a side of her that he had never seen before and it amazed him. *She's so peaceful. She looks 10 years younger. It must be her new friend. Remarkable,* he thought as he handed Peter's medical chart to Alex. "He's two floors up. I have two sets of scrubs here for you so I can sneak you into ICU."

Alex nodded, took a set of scrubs, and handed the other set to Patty. "Good. When will the specialist be here?" she asked.

"In about two hours. Come along, gentlemen, let's give the ladies some privacy to change," he suggested, as he led the other two out of the room.

*****

Three people in scrubs and two ambulance drivers entered the ICU unit and followed Sam to Peter's room. Alex nodded to the two policemen who were guarding the door at her request.

The patient was already wide awake when he heard all the footsteps enter his room. He felt a gentle hand enclose his own and knew instantly whose it was. "This is not your fault, my friend," he assured Alex.

"Then whose is it?" Alex felt tears sting her eyes at the sight of the bandage wrapped around his eyes.

Peter shook his head. "Well, it isn't yours. Its Julie's...I mean Julia Zarrelli's, of course. You and Vito both warned me. I was very stupid. I...well, I should..."

"Stop." Alex shook her head at her friend in wonder. "How on earth can you be blaming yourself? Why the hell aren't you blaming me?"

Peter smiled and shrugged his shoulders; "I'm the one who pulled that wire. How stupid could I have been? I knew whom I was dealing with, and I still charged in like a fool. I guess its all perspective. You warned me, and all you've done since this all started was try to protect everyone. How could I blame you?"

Alex was so upset she was having trouble breathing. She felt a warm, protective arm encircle her waist. She looked down and met the concerned green eyes, shaking her head, showing only Patty her vulnerability.

So the small blonde did what she knew she had to, she jumped in to help. "Alex is feeling very badly, Peter. She thinks she should have seen this coming, that she shouldn't have left Julia and her uncle at Toys." Looking up into tear-filled blue eyes, she said, "You're not being very logical, love. You said yourself that it's all circumstantial evidence. We don't even have proof that they did this. You should listen to your own words: this is the Zarrelli's' fault, not yours."

119

She then gently rubbed Alex's stomach with one hand and with her other she caressed her blinded friend's cheek, trying to comfort them both.

"Peter, Alex has arranged for an eye specialist to see you. Maybe he can help you...well..."

"So I'll see again?" He finished for her quietly, but there was little hope in his voice. It was heart breaking for both women, who only knew Peter as upbeat.

"Yes, that's exactly what he is going to do," said Alex.

There was no uncertainty in her voice though it was barely raised above a whisper.

"It's a nice gesture, Alex but..."

"It is perfectly possible," interrupted Sam. "I know the doctor, and he is the best in the business. You have an excellent chance."

The room was very quiet as they all sent up silent prayers that Sam's words would come true.

*****

Alex had decided they would wait at the mansion for the results of the tests that the specialist had run. They were trying to unwind watching an old movie on TV when the footman Jonathan came in. Alex looked up from her comfortable position with a look that told the man that the interruption had better be justified.

He understood the warning, but knew that his news was important, so he went on with what he had to say. "Ma'am, Detective Jaust is here to see you."

Alex smirked and shook her head, "I knew he would be coming around after what happened to Peter. Please send him right in, Jonathan."

The tall man nodded and bowed slightly. "Very well, Ma'am."

Alex chuckled as she looked into an equally amused set of green eyes. She bent down and kissed Patty's forehead, then whispered, "Why do I feel like I'm in the middle of murder mystery whenever I speak to a member of my household staff? I swear that Dad had to be deeply influenced by old movies and decided to staff this place with people who most closely resembled the characters he liked the best," she said laughing to the woman nestled against her chest.

Patty laughed, too, and then she gently slapped Alex's arm. "Oh you! I think they are all really sweet."

"They are, or they wouldn't still be here. I do like them, but I feel like Morticia from the Addam's Family."

"Should I speak French?"

"Mmm, yeah, that would be nice, but wait 'til old Jaust leaves," she said, tickling the smaller woman and laughing at her contagious giggles.

"Well, walking into room full of laughter can't be a bad thing, right?" asked the detective, leaning against the doorway to the room.

"Right. What have you found out, old boy?"

Alex motioned for Patty to sit up, which she did immediately.

"Patty, I think you remember my old sparring partner from the police station? Old boy, you remember the love of my life, don't you? You are doing your utmost to protect her, right?" she asked meaningfully.

"Yes, and you damn well know it. We talked about her for an hour and a half." Seeing the young woman blush, he smiled. "Don't worry, it was all good, Patty."

"How could it not be?" asked Alex sincerely, and she watched with amusement as her beloved's blush deepened. She bent close and whispered to her, "You are so beautiful when you blush, you know that, don't you?"

Patty's reply was to hide her face against Alex's shoulder. Alex smiled as she hugged her love and tipped a wink to her old friend. He winked back.

"It seems as if the love of your life is shy. Unlike a certain blue eyed vixen who shall remain nameless."

Alex stroked Patty's hair, looking completely besotted to Jaust's astonishment.

"I know that. It's one of the many things I love about her." She gently kissed the crown of the head beneath her and leaned against the arm of the couch, bringing her love with her. Then her gaze changed, hardening slightly as she looked at the man across the room. She continued to cuddle Patty lovingly, but the look was the old Alex, and that threw Jaust for a loop.

"Ah, that is my cue to get down to business. Well, we have had the suspects under tight surveillance—both visual and audio. They have been keeping away from each other since the explosion. Uncle Nutcase has called Niece Wacko at least three times; each time she hung up on him. It seems that old crazy wants to get their master plan underway now…"

"Which is?" growled Alex. The two women had moved while he had been talking and were now tensely sitting side by side on the edge of the couch.

Jaust swallowed a couple of time, then replied quietly, "He wants to kidnap Patty. It's still their major playing card, Alex. They haven't been able to get near her since you're with her 24 and 7, but Julia feels sooner or later you'll have to let her out of your sight. Since Julia thinks that you don't yet know it's her, she believes that when you do let your guard down, Patty will be an open target. She told her uncle to wait it out."

"Well, they can wait 'til the goddamn cows come home. I'm not letting Patty out of my sight!" Alex pulled Patty close, hugging her protectively. Patty snuggled close and gently rubbed her hand against Alex's back.

Jaust nodded. "That's what I thought your reaction would be, old girl. I do have an idea, though."

"What?"

"You could be the lure, Alex, and…"

"No!"

Patty's arms now tightened, holding Alex even closer. She looked at Jaust and said with a strength that surprised him, "I will not allow Alex to sacrifice herself for me."

Alex pulled back and gently brushed some hair out of the now-angry green eyes. She cupped Patty's cheeks and looked deep into those hypnotic eyes, then said very quietly, "I would do anything for you."

Patty now had tears gently trickling out of her eyes, and she cried, "Please, Alex, don't. There has got to be another way. It took so long to find you, I can't lose you now."

Alex wiped away the tears and then pulled Patty close again. With her own eyes closed, she said quietly, "You won't lose me, love, I promise."

When her eyes opened and met Jaust's, they were blazing at him with icy blue anger. He actually took a step back from the murderous look.

"Whoa, you two. I have no intention of allowing Alex to sacrifice herself. All I want is for Alex to lure Julia to Toys. You won't be in any danger, Alex; I will arrange everything."

"Please," cried Patty, still terrified.

"Shh, it's okay. That's not what I want to do. Calm down, I have other plans. Look at me," She chucked her under the chin until she met teary green eyes.

"I have a much better idea, one to get real evidence against those two and keep you happy."

"Really?" Patty asked in a whisper.

"Really."

Forgetting Jaust was even there, she brought their lips together in a passionate kiss. Embarrassed, the man left the room to give his friends some privacy.

*****

Alex and Patty arrived by ambulance again and were whisked up to the private room that Alex had arranged for Peter. She had made sure that he had the best of everything, including around-the-clock police protection. They were waiting quietly with Peter for the specialist who would be coming with the results of all the tests he had performed the day before.

There was a gentle knock, and the policeman opened the door for the tall, distinguished looking man. They all looked at him anxiously. He smiled kindly at them, then took Peter's hand.

"I have very good news, young man: you will see. And I do not make promises I cannot keep. It will be a slow progression to regain your full vision, and you'll never be allowed to fly a plane..."he joked, as the room burst into a joyful din.

Peter enjoyed listening to all the happiness around him. He reached out and took Alex's hand and said very quietly, "I wish I could see you right now, Alex. I know you have big smile and tears flowing down your cheeks. I am so grateful to you..."

Alex hugged him and replied quietly back, "Why would you be grateful to me? If it wasn't for me..."

"If it wasn't for you, I would be blind for life."

"If it wasn't for me, you would have never been hurt in the first place."

He reached up and wiped the tears that he could feel dripping onto his own skin.

"Oh, Alex, how can you know that? Maybe it was fate I'd lose my sight for a while. Maybe I'm meant to learn something from it, like maybe I should think before I do something stupid next time."

"Don't you dare blame yourself for this..." she growled protectively.

"Well, I don't want you blaming yourself, either. You know damn well only two people are to blame, and I know you will bring them to justice. I am mad at myself for hiring her. I am mad at myself for not seeing through her charade. I am not at all mad you, Alex. Alex?" He could feel her body shuddering.

"Patty, are you here? Please help her."

Patty, who was talking to Vito, heard Peter and saw that Alex was now silently sobbing, so she rushed to the aggrieved woman's side. She pulled her into her arms and hugged her tightly, whispering, "Are you okay?"

Alex nodded and rested her head on top of Patty's. In a gruff voice, Alex said, "Yeah...I guess. I'm so damn lucky to have people who love me despite all my faults."

Patty snuggled closer and whispered, "Because of all your strengths."

They stayed cuddled for a while, then Patty pulled back and gently wiped the tears from the red-rimmed blue eyes. She smiled at the distraught woman and asked, "Would you like some coffee? There's a machine right down the hall."

"Yes, that would be very nice. Send the policeman for it, will you, love?"

"Well, actually, I was going to go. I have to go to the bathroom, and the machine is right next to it."

"I'll go with you."

Patty caressed Alex's cheek and said sweetly, "I'm a big girl. I can go to the bathroom all by myself. Its only three doors away and the coffee machine is even closer than that. Besides the policeman is right there. I'll be okay."

Alex struggled with her instincts; she knew it wasn't a good idea to let Patty out of her sight. The threat was still out there and very real. She also knew that the policeman was right there, and both the bathroom and the coffee machine were in his sight. She reluctantly relented.   Okay...but be very careful."

Patty rolled her eyes and crossed them just to relax Alex and make her smile, and then ran to the bathroom. She really had to go.

*****

Patty left the bathroom and was waiting for the steaming liquid to pour into the first cup when she felt a presence behind her. In the reflection of the glass front on the machine, she could see a big orderly slowly approaching her. There was something about him that made her nervous. She looked carefully: he had a cloth loosely hanging from one hand, and he was wearing a surgical mask but no scrubs. It all clicked instantly, and she grabbed the cup of coffee and threw it in the man's face. Screaming, she ran toward the policeman as fast as she could.

The policeman pulled out his weapon and was about to put Patty protectively behind him when a figure streaked out of the private room. Alex instantly put herself between Patty and the approaching assailant.

"Well, well, Mr. Zarrelli. Don't you think it's about time you picked on someone your own size?" Alex growled with a savage look in her eyes.

The huge bear of man was still trying to wipe the hot coffee from his face when it registered that Alex knew who he was. He growled and attacked the woman who had killed his family. Ignoring the policeman, he charged at the tall woman. She easily sidestepped his attack and placed a perfect sidekick against his right ribcage, causing him to double over in agony.

Alex turned and gathered Patty into a loving hug as the policeman twisted the man's hands behind his back to cuff them.

"Not a very elegant performance, was it, love?" she whispered as she looked deeply into Patty's eyes to make sure she was okay. Then she brought their lips together for a deep loving kiss.

"You bitch!" The big man screamed as the policeman propelled him toward the elevator. He would be taken to the jail ward, and then Jaust would be called in to take him to the police station.

Alex lifted her head and shook it.

"Now that's really original," she called back calmly. Then she looked at Patty and asked quietly, "Are you sure you're okay? Did he get near you at all?"

"I saw him in the machine. I threw the coffee at his face then I ran as fast as I could. I'm fine; it's just that..." she shook her head ashamedly, "I should have listened to you. I am so sorry…"

"Shhh, stop that. I'm very proud of you. You did very well," Alex said to the upset woman, a deep, shining pride lighting her eyes.

Patty's head tilted to the side and Alex couldn't help but think how cute she looked when she was confused. "I did? How did I?"

"Mmmhmm, yes you did very well. He was a professional, believe it or not. And you, my little one, stopped him right in his tracks. You stopped him and alerted us that you were in danger. It was very, very well done."

Patty blushed and snuggled her head against Alex's shoulder, murmuring, "It was pure instinct…"

"Perfect instinct. Really, sweetheart, I am so proud of you I could just burst." Alex said, kissing the bright red cheek with a loving smile. "But, I think we had better leave for the cabin right now . Once Julia finds out about her uncle's unsuccessful attempt, she will try to come up with a counterattack." Green frightened eyes looked up at her.

Alex winked back and said very calmly, "Don't worry; I've got a few ideas."

*****

Julia stormed through her small apartment in a homicidal rage. She had already thrown every breakable thing within reach, but nothing seemed to assuage the anger she felt. The moment she got the call from her uncle, she could feel it begin burning in her stomach. She told him to keep his big mouth shut about her and to say he was acting on his own. She also told the old fool not worry—that she would get him an attorney, since blood was blood.

"Stupid, egotistical asshole! He attempts to kidnap her right in front of a damn cop! How idiotic can be you be, you stupid fuckhead! What an imbecile. I can't believe we are related," she ranted, as she threw a gold-framed picture of her beloved father across the room shattering the glass against a wall.

"Okay, Alex, it's time to take the gloves off. It's going to be you and me to the death!"

*****

Alex and Patty arrived back up at the cabin well before dark. Alex turned off the ignition and looked at the sleeping woman beside her. *You are so precious to me. I am going to protect you at all costs. I will keep my promise to you, my darling, but if this comes down to a choice between you and Julia, I will not hesitate to protect you any way I can,* she thought grimly, gently brushing the soft blonde hair. She sighed and lowered her hand to Patty's shoulder, shaking her gently.

Sleepy green eyes opened and Patty mumbled tiredly, "I take it we're home?"

Alex smiled tenderly and nodded her head. "You take it right, sweetheart. Would you like me to carry you into the cabin?" she asked with lopsided grin, causing the small blonde to laugh and shake her head. "No, I think I can make it under my own power."

Patty got out of the car and stretched her back 'til she heard a loud, satisfying crack. Alex chuckled as she came around the car to stand next to her. She slid her arm around her waist and gently guided her toward the door. "How about a nice massage tonight to ease the strain?"

"Only if I can return the favor."

"That's a deal, little one."

*****

Patty wasn't able to keep her end of the bargain, because under Alex's gentle loving caresses she fell deeply asleep, as the tall woman had known she would.

Alex slipped out of bed and put on her robe to go down the hall to the living room to call Uncle Vito. Once all her plans had been set in motion, she slipped out of her robe and slid back under the covers to cuddle against a still sound a sleep blonde.

She was on her back with hands under head, looking up at the vaulted ceiling and totally unable to sleep. She listened with a quiet thankfulness to the soft breathing of the woman beside her. Her thoughts would not let her rest.

I could have lost you today, my love. I am so grateful you were able to think so fast under the circumstances, but this is unacceptable to me. I need to know you're safe. I want you by my side forever. I have to end this thing with the Zarrelli's and get out. I need to be free of this so I can concentrate on you and our future. Once this is done, I will hand it all over to Vito and I'm free. I want to go away for a while: somewhere nice and quiet like it is up here, with no past—only us and our future. I want to discover every detail about you. I want us just to relax and have fun; I don't want to be plagued with doubts and worries. When we come home, it will just be Toys I'd be responsible for, so I can lead a peaceful, legal life with the woman I love. That's my real destiny. She sighed and looked out the window toward the woods and lake. *Please, God, make it so. My Patty deserves nothing less.*

Alex rolled over onto her side and spooned her love; she heard a contented little sigh from Patty and smiled. She brought her breathing to the same rhythm as her beloved and fell instantly asleep.

*****

Alex awoke the next morning to the feel of gentle caresses against her stomach and small jets of air blowing softly against her belly button. One blue opened to see that she was exposed all the way down to just below her waist. Two green eyes were concentrating very hard on the exposed area. The other eye opened and she smiled at the other woman.

"May I ask you what you're doing?"

The green eyes lifted sheepishly to meet the amused blue and Patty said, "Well, I couldn't think of another way to gently wake you, and I still owe you a massage."

Alex laughed softly and shook her head.

"Where would you like to start it?" she croaked, as her throat suddenly went very dry.

"Mmm, I think it would be safer to start on your back. We may never get out of bed if I start on your stomach," said the smaller woman, trying for a lecherous grin but only succeeding in a delighted smile.

Alex laughed and bent to kiss the smaller woman on the cheek. Then she turned over so her back was facing her love. She looked over her shoulder and said with a smirk, "It's all yours."

Patty smiled and got the oil from the bedside table. She then proceeded to ease the tension out of every nook and cranny she found beneath her fingers.

As Alex slowly relaxed under the gentle rhythm of the massage, she found herself falling deeply asleep. It was several hours later that she found herself alone in bed, fully covered by the soft blanket. There was no sign of Patty anywhere.

She got out of bed and glanced at the clock to see that the time was now 3 p.m. Her eyes widened at the realization that she had slept all day. She left the bedroom calling for her little one.

"In here," was Patty's reply from the kitchen.

Alex found Patty in the midst of making a large meal, "Are we expecting a huge party of people?"

"Well, two guests anyway, Uncle Vito and Jaust will be here at 5 p.m. You have 2 hours to shower and change," she said with a smirk, knowing how fast Alex could change clothes.

Alex smiled and shook her head at Patty's calm voice. "I think I can handle it. What did you do all day after you gave me that sleeping pill disguised as a massage?"

"Well, I slept too. Then I cleaned the place a little. Then I talked to Uncle Vito for an hour and found out about them coming up. So I cleaned the guestroom and put clean linen on both beds in there. Then I came in here and got cracking on dinner." She smiled proudly over her shoulder at Alex.

Alex's smile became blinding as she listened to her love's list grow and grow.

"Come here, you. I need my morning hello."

Patty gladly went into the tall woman's embrace, and they kissed deeply. Alex was amazed as always by the wonderful sense of peace she felt when she was in Patty's arms. She pulled back slightly so she could see into the hypnotic eyes and said with a crooked grin, "So, in other words, you've been quite busy. Why did you let me sleep so long?"

She then softly kissed the forehead that was right under her and kept going down the beloved face until she reached her chin, then her neck.

Patty enjoyed the attention, then pulled back slightly and smiled into the wicked blue eyes. "Come on, Alex, you were exhausted. You drove us all the way up here, and I know you stayed up all night worrying. I thought you needed someone to watch over you for a change, and I decided that I'd take the job."

Patty's arms tightened around Alex's waist, her hands stroking the strong back, relaxing the tall woman further.

"You've got the job...for life. Now, if you keep this up, you will put me to sleep on the kitchen floor. What kind of impression do you think that would make on our guests? Is there anything I can do to help you?"

She pulled away a bit more, but still kept Patty within the circle of her arms.

Patty shook her head.

"You never cease to amaze me, do you know that? Well, if you insist, you could help me by tossing that salad."

Alex kissed the pert little nose. "You got it, boss."

*****

At 5 p.m. sharp, the two men arrived. Vito had driven Jaust up and, in an attempt to protect Alex, he had blindfolded the policeman for the entire ride.

Jaust allowed the old man to cover his eyes with a soft cloth with good grace. He knew that Vito was trying to protect Alex, and he found it very amusing. He knew pretty much where he was, anyway; he had an excellent sense of direction.

Alex was very touched by Vito's precaution, and amused when her friend had laughingly told her and Patty the story. She couldn't resist teasing her uncle. As she hugged him in thanks for being so cautious, she asked with a tiny giggle, "Got to keep these coppers guessing, huh, Unc?"

Vito took the ribbing in the spirit it was given. Knowing that Alex needed the distraction, he laughed too.

"Next time, I'll let that ingrate over there follow a trail of bread crumbs," he grumbled glowering at the amused detective.

This caused more laughter all around. Patty recovered first and said quietly, "Dinner will be ready soon. Would you all like to start on the delicious salad that Alex made?"

"You cooked?" asked Vito, shocked.

"Unc, you don't cook salad. All I did was simply take the ingredients that Patty laid out for me and tossed them in the bowl. Poof, you have salad. It's not a big deal," she said with lopsided grin as she took her seat at the head of the table.

Jaust looked around the cabin as he sat down, and was impressed with how warm and cozy it looked.

"This is nice, Alex. Did you do the decorating?"

Alex smiled proudly and nodded, "Mostly. The newer, prettier additions were introduced very recently, huh, Patty?" she answered, trying to catch the blushing blonde's eyes, which were well hidden beneath her bangs.

Patty took a big bite of salad and then, desperately trying to change the subject, said, "This is really good, Alex. You did a wonderful job."

This caused the two men to laugh unexpectedly, and Patty to put her fork down and say fitfully, "Um, I think dinner is ready. Excuse me."

With a wide smile on her face, Alex put her napkin on the table and said quietly, "Excuse me, too."

She followed Patty into the kitchen and leaned against the door jamb, watching the expert cook pull the lasagna out of the oven. "You know, I think you are absolutely ravishing when you blush like that."

"Yes, I do know that, since you make me do it all the time." She smiled into twinkling blue eyes and said, "Now make yourself useful and take the garlic bread out of the microwave."

"Yes, ma'am."

Two calm, happy women brought dinner to the table, where it was enjoyed by the whole party. After the cook was complimented to the point that she blushed beet red again, they all went to the living room to have the meeting they all dreaded but knew was absolutely necessary.

*****

Patty and Alex were seated on the couch, cuddled very close to each other. Alex's arms were around Patty's waist, holding her tight, and Patty was leaning back against Alex's comfortingly warm embrace. The two men each took a chair and waited for Alex to signal that she was ready.

When she nodded slightly, Jaust began by simply looking at his friend and saying, "Everything is set up just the way you want it, Alex."

"Good."

"What is your plan?" asked Patty quietly.

Alex brought her hand up and ran her fingers through the soft blonde hair. She leaned her head on top of Patty's and said quietly, "You remember that Julia has been under surveillance?"

"Yes," replied Patty in a suddenly frightened voice.

"Well, I just put out a small tidbit of gossip that I will be in the office all day tomorrow, from early in the morning to late at night. It's the end of the fiscal quarter, so it wouldn't be unusual for me. In fact, before I met you, I rarely seemed to leave my office. What I'm hoping is that if the bitch thinks I'm alone, she will attack me..."

"No!"

Patty pulled back so fast that she almost knocked Alex off the couch.   Alex pulled Patty to her by her waist and said soothingly, "Shh, easy love, easy. I have no intention of setting myself up for a hit. All I want to do is make her think that I am."

"But, Alex, you'll be there all alone and vulnerable to..."

"She'll only appear to be alone, Patty. I promise you she won't be alone for a minute and definitely not vulnerable," said the detective, trying to help soothe his new friend's fears.

Alex nodded and kissed Patty's cheek.

"Shh, that's right. It will only look like I'm alone in my office. I won't be, sweetheart. I'll either have Old Jaust there or a policewoman with me at all times. I will be under the eye of the camera which you and Unc can monitor. Tommy will pretend to be ill, but in reality he will be watching the bitch. This was on my insistence. I prefer real people to technology when my life's at stake. The policewoman will pretend to be my temporary secretary. Oh, by the way, old boy, she'd better be convincing, 'cause Julia's no fool and she will check her out."

The detective smiled knowingly.

"She will be very convincing because Cindy worked her way through college doing secretarial work. She knows the job very well. In fact, she is a great help at the precinct when we can't the computer to cooperate on Excel or Lotus."

Alex grinned approvingly.

She hugged Patty tighter and then looked at her friend

gratefully. "Good man. Anyway, what I'm trying to get across is that I will appear to be her target, but I am not going to be a target. Okay?"

Patty was still scared, but she understood it had to be done. Much to everyone's relief, especially Alex's, she nodded her head. "What about me?"

"You are staying right here with Uncle Vito…"

"No, Alex…"

Shhh, It's going to be all right. You'll be able to keep tabs on me all day. You will get to watch me on that new video equipment that Jaust put in my office this morning. I will never be out of your sight for a minute."

She leaned very close and whispered with an embarrassed chuckle, "You'll even watch my private moments." She glanced across the room at her chuckling uncle saying out loud, "Uncle Vito insisted that the cameras cover my private bathroom, but I'm counting on you to make sure I retain my privacy. Okay, love?"

Patty eyes widened in shock. "Of course."

Vito was very amused by Patty's innocent reaction, and laughed.

"Listen to you. I used to change your diapers, you little brat."

"Well I've changed a bit since then, Unc." They all laughed, feeling a little of the tension leave the room.

"Alex, do you think she'll risk trying to do something to you?"

"Yes, sweetheart, I do. Don't you worry, though; I have a few interesting plans for the clever Julia. Believe me, the only one who will be unpleasantly surprised is the one who deserves to be," said Alex with a feral look glinting in her suddenly icy blue eyes.

Chapter Eleven
The Trap

Alex was in her own office working at her own desk on her very own computer. It all appeared so normal, but she knew it wasn't. She glanced up at the tiny hole over head where she knew a camera was carefully picking up her every move.

She sighed as her eyes flicked back to the spreadsheet on the computer screen. It was not a happy girlfriend that she'd left that morning. In fact, the feeling of melancholy caused by the confrontation was still very much with her as she tried to concentrate on the figures in front of her.

They had already loaded the car for the trip back to the city. Uncle Vito would meet them at the mansion where she would drop off Patty, and Alex would then head into the office all alone.

"Alex isn't there another way?" asked Patty as they ate breakfast at the cabin.

"No, sweetheart, there isn't. We have already discussed this. I know how you feel. I know you think I'm taking too much of a risk, but...we need this to end. We can't have it hanging

over us like this. I want to be free to..." *Alex turned away from the person who meant everything to her as unwanted tears fell down her cheeks*

Patty got up and came around the table to stand beside the crying woman. She gently turned the proud head back toward her and dried the tears with her fingers. The tears kept falling despite the fact Alex was trying to control them, and this broke Patty's heart.

"Shh, stop trying so hard. Its okay, you don't have to say any more. You don't owe me any explanation..."

"Yes, I do!" Alex exclaimed, throwing her arms around her beloved and pulling her as close as possible. The next words were whispered in a low passionate voice, so low that Patty had to strain to hear her. "You are my whole world. I owe you everything, sweetheart. I owe you my love, loyalty, and my life. I would die for you in a heartbeat." Feeling Patty's body stiffen, she hurried on. "But I'll do better than that this time; I will live. I will win this fight and my freedom, so I can plan and create the kind of life I know we both need and deserve. A life of peace. I want us to be happy and content with each other forever. I love you so much." Alex felt tender lips kiss hers and she kissed her love back with passion, love, and pure devotion.

*****

"Ma'am?" Blue eyes popped open to see the policewoman Cindy smiling at her. Alex shook her head as she realized that she had allowed herself to drift off with her thoughts. Knowing how dangerous that was, she could have kicked herself. She had to remember to focus on the job at hand and not let her mind stray.

"Yes, Cynthia?"

The other woman nodded slightly and said quietly, "You asked to be reminded when it was 10 a.m."

Alex nodded and smiled wickedly at the young woman saying, "Yep, I sure did. Thanks."

"My pleasure, ma'am," the young woman said with a wink, as she went out the door, closing it firmly behind her.

Once closed off from the rest of the company again, she whistled and said, "Well, my little bird just flew into the cage, did she?"

She turned back toward her desk and started to fidget with the spreadsheet on the screen. The room was safe: she'd had it and the phone swept; but she had told Cindy to leave the door open so any mikes at Tommy's desk would pick up pre-formatted conversations. The signal for Julia's arrival was that Cindy would speak to Alex as if she was being reminded of important engagement. Then, once she knew her tormentor was in the office, Julia would be under constant scrutiny—not only by Alex, but also by the police in an office down the hall.

Alex flicked on a tiny monitor for a camera that had been hidden on a shelf so she could keep tabs on her enemy. *Damn her! She acts so normal. She just puts her stuff away and gets a cup of coffee,* thought Alex as she fiddled with a paper clip on her desk. *Do something already! I need to get on with my life. Move!*

The phone on her desk rang, interrupting her thoughts for a minute as she glanced down at it. She picked it up, saying efficiently, "Alex." Her eyes flicked back to the monitor where, much to her annoyance, the small redhead was starting her normal business day.

"Alexa, calm down," Vito said soothingly on the phone.
A tiny smirk appeared on her face, replacing the grim expression that had been firmly planted there seconds before. "What makes you think I'm not?"

"I do know you pretty well, damn it. You're as jittery as a goddamned bird; now calm down." He chuckled and then said softly, "I think your Patty has gnawed off all her fingernails watching you."

The moment Alex heard Patty's name, her face brightened

considerably. She suddenly looked happy just hearing the sweet syllables.

"Is she available?"

Vito laughed, "Is the Pope Catholic? Of course she is."

The next voice she heard calmed her right down, bringing a sweet peace to her pounding heart.,"Alex?"

"Hi."

"Hi, are you okay?"

"Of course I am. Don't I look okay?"

"Yes, you look beautiful. You also look very nervous. I see it and so does Vito, but don't worry, no one else would. It's just little things that you pick up when you love someone."

"Oh? Like what?"

"Your jaw is very tight, you're playing with your hair, you're playing with your third paper clip, and you keep switching screens on the computer before you really look at the page..."

Alex laughed. "Okay, I get the idea. I...uh...I just want to get this over with already. I want to get the hell out of here and back to you."

"I want that, too."

"Patty...when this is all over...I...uh..." She was interrupted by a knock on the door. "Hold on a minute, love." She put Patty on hold and said, "Yes?"

"Ma'am, the package is on the move," said Cindy, indicating that Julia left her office.

Alex's eyes flicked to the monitor, and her expression changed in an instant to that of the head of Murder Inc. In an angry growl she said, "Yep, the package appears to be gone."

"I believe it would be best to meet it."

Alex nodded. "Yep, you're right. Um...hold on a minute." Then she turned back to her phone, picked up the receiver, and said softly to Patty, "I'll call you back as soon as I can."

"Be careful, Alex."

"I will. Talk to you in a bit."

She hung up, her eyes staring at the phone for a second.

When she looked up, her eyes were of pure ice, which sent shivers down the young police officer's spine as Alex said in angry growl, "Okay, Cindy, let's get this goddamned package sorted out once and for all."

*****

Julia was ecstatic. Her target was at the company all alone, without Tommy or any of her other protectors, no one to watch over her except one pretty little temp who didn't know beans about her boss or what she did. She had watched in the break room as the sweet little thing with the glasses slipping off her nose introduced herself to them all with a big, bright smile.

This is so great. I'll just wait 'til the sweet little temp takes her first break, and then...boom! Bye bye Alex, forever! the redheaded woman thought as she casually strolled toward the executive office of Toys, Inc. She was now in position in the break room, where she could watch Alex's front door and then slip in through the side door when the girl left. She sipped her coffee and quietly waited.

*****

Patty and Vito waited in Alex's den, watching through the monitor as Alex and the police tried to pinpoint Julia in the complex maze of offices. When they spotted the redhead, Patty's grip tightened on Vito's wrist.

Vito gently patted the little hand and said, "Don't worry, little one, that idiot has no idea who she's up against." He tenderly turned her head until he could look the scared girl right in the eyes as he continued. "You know the sweet, soft side of my Alexa, right?" Smiling slightly, Patty nodded her head. He smiled back.

"That is because you bring out the best in her. All her goodness just comes pouring out when she sees you. You are blessing to her because when you came into her life you allowed her to finally become fully herself. But, my young friend, she is still a very formidable woman, even more so when she is protecting those she loves. As much as she hates that side of her personality, there is no one more deadly then my Alexa, once provoked. This woman's biggest mistake was in targeting you and me. We are Alexa's family. She is now like a female tiger protecting her cubs—a very deadly creature."

Patty's eye widened as she realized that what Vito had said was absolutely true. Vito's eyes had gone back to the screen as he watched his niece consult with the police. He had a fatherly arm protectively around Patty's shoulders, but wasn't paying attention to the signals the girl was now sending out.

Patty was reflecting on what he had just told her and what she knew from Alex herself. When Alex had given her the files on her past, Patty had read them but until now, it hadn't totally sunk in. She had never seen Alex that way; she was protective, yes, but never vicious or deadly. Suddenly she experienced something that really stunned her: she was excited and turned on by this other side. She took a deep breath and opened her eyes.

She looked at the screen and her eyes widened. Alex was gone. "Uncle Vito, where did Alex go?"

"She went up into the access way in her bathroom. Were you daydreaming, little one?" Vito asked, rather surprised since the green eyes never had left the screen.

"Um, something like that," admitted Patty, very embarrassed. She was beet red, and Vito wondered what was going through his young friend's thoughts.

*****

Alex went into her bathroom, pulled out the screen covering the access way, then very gracefully pulled herself up into it. She had dressed with care in the morning, knowing she had to appear business as usual to fool Julia. Black leggings and a tank top were topped off with red floral silk jacket and matching pumps. She had her hair pulled back into a silver barrette, and she wore matching earrings and a bracelet. Hidden from view were the tennis shoes in her briefcase.

As soon as the office had been swept for sound devices, she took off her heels, which was not unusual as she liked to run around her office barefoot, slipping her sneakers under the desk so she could put them on in a hurry. Before she went into her bathroom she took off her jacket and jewelry, and slipped her sneakers on. She was ready for battle.

As she carefully crawled down the long access way she thought, *Sometimes I really wish I hadn't inherited Dad's height. It would have been so much easier if I was petite like Mom.* She chuckled silently as she slid her long frame toward the break room thinking, *I hope my old friend remembered to lock the side door.*

*****

Cindy, meanwhile, confronted Julia in a friendly manner like any fellow secretary would. She entered the break room quickly and blocked the exit so that Julia had no time to retreat.

"Hi, my name is Cynthia, what's yours?"

"My name is Julie," she said impatiently.

Cindy seemed not to notice as she went on, "Nice to meet you. Where do you work? I work for Miss Bennett. Only temporarily of course," she said with a giggle pushing her glasses up her nose.

Very temporary, thought Julia with an inward smile. "Do you know where you go from here?"

"Who knows. That's what I like about being a temp, you never know what to expect," she said shrugging her shoulders, then she took a long sip from her coffee.

"How do you like the Boss Lady? I hear she's tough to work for."

"Oh, I think she's great, just full of surprises, "said Cindy with an innocent look. Out of the corner of her eye, she saw the grid moving silently away from the vent and up toward the absolutely still figure behind it.

"Really?" Julia said as if bored; she wanted to get back into position. She had no idea what was happening behind the stupid temp.

"Yes. Well, I'd better get back to the boss. See you," Cindy said with a pleasant grin. *Yeash, Alex, you move like a panther,* she thought as she walked back to tell her boss that the mouse was in play. *All we have to do is wait for the cat to meow.*

"See you," said Julia, rolling her eyes. She leaned against the door and was once again staring at the exit across the hall as a figure silently lowered herself down from the grid behind her, looking at the redhead's back with Cheshire Cat grin.

*****

"Good Morning, Julia," purred the tall woman from behind the startled redhead.

Julia spun, her expression going quickly from shock to anger.

"How?"

"How what? How did I know you were in here? How did I get here? How did I figure out it was innocent little you? Ah, so many questions, so little time," Alex said sweetly as she leaned against the wall under the grid. Her arms were crossed in front of her, and she had a deceptively calm expression on her face. She looked tall, cool, and deadly, no worse for wear from her little trip down the tiny access way.

Julia looked at the sleek woman all in black, her thoughts flicking involuntarily to a panther stalking its prey. She angrily shook her head and thought desperately, *I'm a tiger and she is my prey.*

She had an angry snarl on her face as she asked viciously, "So, how is your sweet little girl friend?"

"Safe."

"And Peter?"

Alex face quickly flashed to anger as she growled, "Sighted, no thanks to you."

"To be honest with you Alex, I like Peter. I am very glad he's going to be okay. He was just a means to an end. You know that the ends always justifies the means."

"No, that's where you're totally wrong. It does not. I will admit I have committed a number of wrongs in my life, but I have never gone after some innocent victim just to get under the skin of my real target. You're lower than low, even in our profession. Peter is a good, honest man, a non-player. When you went after him, you broke the unwritten rules and you know it." Alex hadn't moved an inch during this angry speech, but Julia felt like the wagons were circling her.

"When the means leads me to this moment, to the death of a most hated enemy, then it's worth it."

"Why exactly am I your enemy?"

"You killed my family."

"Your family killed my father and ruined my life. If it hadn't been for his murder, I would have never gotten into this miserable business at all. I'd say we were even…"

"Never! I want to see you in your grave!"

Alex shook her head. She was still calm but lethal in appearance. She kept Julia in her sight as she casually walked to the coffee and poured herself a cup. "Why? Your father killed my father, why exactly are we different, Julia?"

"You survived, in fact, you prospered. Look at you. This place, the way you live. You are so damned happy and…"

Alex laughed grimly and Julia's eyes widened in shock, "You think I'm happy because of the money I have?"

"Of course!"

"Well you're wrong. I see you really didn't do any research on your target at all. Shame on you, that's standard procedure. Well, I'll help you out. I never had a single happy day after my father died 'til I met and fell in love with Patty. Money did nothing for me. I always had it and I was never happy. Love is what finally brought me happiness. It's made me want to change my ways and live the kind of life I was meant to…"

"Bullshit! You're a murder! How dare you talk of love!" screamed the now hysterical woman.

Alex was very calm as she looked the angry redhead in the eye. "So are you." She sipped her coffee and then put the cup down, "You killed Robby. What did he do to you? I know he was an assassin, but he didn't make a hit against you or your family. He wasn't even around when the vendetta was begun. He was a rookie, easy pickings. Then there were your attempts against people who were not players without any contracts against them simply to get at me and hurt me. People who are good and honest. I could never have done that. I couldn't have allowed any of my people to do that. It's simply wrong. I have only hit on a contract; even during the vendetta we didn't hit kids or innocent woman. You're still alive, so are several of your cousins and aunts because of that policy. I will spend the rest of my life trying to redeem myself for the crimes that I have committed. I may never really be able to, but I will die still trying. You are going to jail for it because you went too far."

"No! I am not going to jail! You are never going to redeem yourself," said Julia sarcastically, with a crazy laugh that made Alex sigh in pity. She had hoped the woman would listen to reason and just turn herself in. She might even be able to get a reduced sentence with an insanity plea.

No, Alex thought, looking into crazed eyes; *She's too far gone. Reason won't work, damn it. Sorry, little one, I did try.*

She sent the thought out toward her beloved, hoping she would get it somehow, in case she was not the one to survive the coming encounter.

"You're going to die, Alex," said Julia, pulling out a pearl handled revolver.

Alex didn't move, she merely leaned back and raised an eyebrow, looking over Julia's shoulder…

Julia laughed wildly at the still figure dressed in black. "I have the drop on you now, Alex. You won't be able to escape me; and I will enjoy my revenge, believe me." The woman's eyes glittered with insanity, and she now seemed to cackle rather than laugh, which made Alex cringe inside.

With pity in her eyes, Alex watched the crazed redhead as a voice behind the smaller woman said, "Don't count on it, Red."

Taken by surprise, Julia turned her head, which gave Alex the opening she had been waiting for. Alex launched into a perfect roundhouse kick, dislodging the gun and sending Julia backwards to land on her back at Tommy's feet. He delivered another blow—a karate chop to the woman's neck. The power of the strike should have incapacitated her, but she was pumped with adrenaline so it had no real effect, except to throw her slightly off balance.

Julia rolled away from her two adversaries and reached for the knife hidden in her high heeled boot. Like a flash of quicksilver, she drew it and slashed straight up Alex's leg all the way to her hip. Blood flowed freely from the wound as Alex fell backwards on to the kitchen floor. With a wild smile, Julia lifted the knife to deliver the deathblow. Then suddenly her vision faded into blackness as hands tightened around her throat and choked the life out of her.

Tommy and a groggy Alex looked up into Val's eyes. Val nodded toward them, smiled grimly, and escaped out the side door just as Jaust and Cindy came in the main door of the small kitchen. As she lost consciousness, the last thing Alex remembered was Jaust cursing his head off.

Chapter Twelve

Recovery

Water... I feel water, thought Alex sleepily as she felt a few little drops hit her skin. *Where the hell am I? Why would water would be falling on me?* She tried to open her eyes but couldn't make them obey her. She did hear someone groan in obvious pain. *Someone is in terrible pain. I wish I could help them.*

*****

Patty was in a chair in Alex's hospital room, leaning over her beloved as tears fell down her cheeks. Droplets fell off her chin and on to Alex's neck and face. Suddenly the tall woman groaned in pain, and she moved her head as if trying to reposition herself. Then there was a twitching around the eyes, and Alex groaned again.

"Alex?" Patty called in grief-stricken voice. She took one of Alex's hands gently kissing the palm.

"Alex, come back to me. Please, you promised you would."

147

*****

As Alex tried to open her eyes, she heard that poor person groan and moan again. Suddenly she heard a soft voice calling her from a great distance.

"Alex?"

Then it was even closer, and she realized that it was her heart calling to her.

"Come back to me, Please, you promised you would."

She knew that it was her soul mate's sweet voice. Her dry lips formed the name as she felt waves of pain crash over her. She felt a kiss on her hand, then on her cheek; and she called out in a shaky voice that she knew was her own. "Patty."

*****

A scratchy voice moaned a name that was barely audible, but the small woman whose life was riding on that voice heard it and rejoiced.

"Patty?"

"Oh, Alex," She cried harder as she kissed her love's cheek. Sleepy, pain-filled blue eyes fluttered open, and a barely visible grin appeared on the injured woman's face, "My beautiful Patty."

"Alex, Oh God....You kept your word..."

"Of course I did," Alex whispered back. She tried, but she couldn't seem to lift her arms as high as she wanted in order to embrace the woman that was crying on the edge of her bed. "Could you kiss me when I'm awake, love? Please?" she whispered, needing to feel Patty beside her far more than any of the stuff being pumped into her by all the tubes she saw attached to her arm.

"Anytime, anywhere," replied Patty passionately as she got up to move closer to Alex and kiss her love on those still tender, swollen lips.

When she pulled back, Alex smiled and said with a slight slur, "Sleepy, Patty."

"I know, love, Go back to sleep."

"Don't leave..." she slurred as she drifted off again.

"No. I never will," said Patty firmly. She sat back down on the chair holding her loves hand waiting for her to wake up once again.

*****

Two days later the wounded executive was whining to her blonde companion. "Come on, my darling, I feel so much better. Can't I go home, please? I can heal the rest of the way there." Alex turned large, pleading, puppy dog eyes on Patty in the hopes that that would work.

"Oh, for God's sake, it's only been two days since you woke up. You were unconscious a whole week from the loss of blood. You're not budging."

"But I feel sooooo much better. You took such good care of me. I'm really ready to go home right now."

"Don't even try to butter me up..."

"Of course I'd never do that. I'll wait until we get home, then I'll do it."

"Alex!"

"Yeash, I'd do it to both of us..."

"You are so impossible!" Patty said. As she turned to stomp out of the room, a long arm grabbed her and pulled her back toward the bed. Alex now had a firm grip around Patty's shoulders and was looking deeply into the big green eyes as she said quietly, "Little one, I need to go home. I need you with me all the time. I can't take this hospital hours stuff anymore. Let me talk to the doctor. I know precisely what buttons to push."

The tall woman had now gotten Patty all the way onto the bed on her good side and was busily undressing her and kissing every inch of skin she could come into contact with. Patty was having a hard time: she was enjoying the kissing, but the undressing part was a bit much for the smaller woman, considering that someone could come in at any time. She was surprised at how fast Alex was getting better, considering the loss of blood she had suffered and how bad the tissue wound was.

The deft hands continued their gentle assault, but Alex did pull back from the kissing for just a second so she could see the blush that she knew was all over Patty's visible skin. Patty smiled and was about to suggest they stop when Alex devilishly pulled those lips to her own and kissed her love passionately.

Just then Jaust and the doctor entered the room. Jaust shook his head and smiled. "Well, Doc, I'd say she is feeling better, wouldn't you?"

"So it would seem. Alex, you are amazing."

Though they had separated as the men had entered the room, Alex wouldn't let Patty leave the circle of her arms. She hugged her close and said to her old friend, "Nope, this one is the amazing one." She then kissed Patty's blushing cheek and said, "You are so damn adorable when you blush."

Patty shifted her head so she was hiding her face against Alex's neck. Alex smiled and stroked the soft blonde hair. She looked at Jaust questioningly. "Well, old friend?"

"The autopsy found that Julia died of a blood clot to the brain. It was a defect from birth, most likely causing her wild behavior. She was a walking time bomb."

Both women looked at the man, shocked. "What?"

"But I actually saw Val…"

"But I thought Val…"

"Yeah, yeah, I know, but she did die of an embolism in the brain. So why don't we let sleeping dogs lie, okay? Val escapes blame on this one, and we have a clean death."

"It's true, Alex, Life is stranger than fiction. I checked the results myself. She would have died then even if Val hadn't been in the room. It was fated by genetics."

"The doc said it could have happened anytime, so we're clear," said Jaust with a smile, knowing that he wouldn't have to do any embarrassing digging.

"Wow!" said Patty not yet over the surprise of it.

Alex was suspicious. "This isn't a set up for me, is it?"

"Nope."

"No fiddling at all?"

"Nope."

"Completely legit?"

"Yep."

"Wow." The two women's eyes met in astonishment.

"The gods do work in mysterious ways, don't they?"

"The gods?" Jaust asked, confused by Patty's weird phrasing.

The girls were still looking only at each other, never straying away from the gaze of their soul mate. Alex smiled and replied very quietly, "Yes, the gods."

*****

Alex and Patty were all set for the getaway that Alex had planned from her hospital bed. She had a phone and a laptop and was driving the nurses crazy, because whenever Patty wasn't there, she was planning their trip.

The day she left the hospital, she handed Patty an envelope with all the information and enjoyed watching the small face look up at her in total amazement.

"I told you that I wanted to take you away when this was all over."

"But what about Toys?"

"Peter will be back in the saddle the day we leave and I will have my cell and laptop if there is an emergency, but I already told him there had better not be."

"Wow! Thank you." There were tears pouring down her cheeks.

"Hey? Why are you crying? I thought you'd like this."

"I do, but you went to a lot of trouble for me and…"

"Shh, stop that train of thought right now, young lady. So, do you want to do it? We could have our joining there, as well as our honeymoon."

Patty was speechless but she kissed her love passionately. Alex accepted the sweet kiss and deepened it. She loved to make her little one happy."

*****

Alex was wearing jeans and a T-shirt, which looked strange to her staff as she strode through the lobby. She went up to the penthouse and Tommy whistled.

"Did Patty ever tell you how hot you look in jeans?"

"Yes, but she likes me better out of them," she replied with a wink, which made Tommy crack up. "Is Unc here?"

"Yep. He's waiting for you."

"Thanks, Tommy." She had started to walk toward her office when Tommy reached out and wrapped a hand around her wrist. "Have a wonderful honeymoon."

"How the hell did you know about that?"

"I did the finals on it, remember?"

Sheepish blue eyes met sparkling brown, and Alex shrugged "Oh, yeah," she said quickly, pulling away and escaping into her office. Tommy sniggered and shook his head, whistling as he went back to work.

"Alexa, you look ready for your trip. Is Patty all set?"

"Yep. Um Unc, thanks for taking care of Fluffy for Patty," said Alex sheepishly about her beloved's white fluff ball of a cat.

"It's no problem. I like her, she's sweet and cuddly, just like Patty. I got used to her when I was watching your place while you girls were up at the cabin."

Alex eyes widened in wonder as she said quietly, "I didn't know that. You took care of Fluffy all that time? Here I thought it was one of the servants."

"I wouldn't do that to Patty, she loves that hair ball. No, I took care of the egotistical feline. So, what time do you leave tomorrow?"

"Two p.m."

"Then: hello new life, right, my Alexa?"

"Yes, Thank God."

*****

They were packed and ready to go, just waiting for Uncle Vito to show up. Cuddling together in the back of the limo, Patty looked up into the warm blue eyes. "Where will we be stopping?"

Alex's face was bright with an indulgent smile as she replied, "I already told you, love, we'll see all of the islands."

"You've been there a couple of times, right?"

"Yep, several, actually."

"Alex, won't you be bored?"

"Nope."

"But, Alex..."

Alex put her hand over the sweet little lips and said very softly, "I could never, ever be bored with you. I mean that. I said it when I first met you, and it's still very true. It will be like seeing it for the first time all over again because I get to see it reflected in your hypnotic green eyes." Then she removed her hand and kissed her love deeply.

Patty melted from the kiss as well as the words and she molded herself into the long body beside her. "Wow!"

Alex looked down at her, amused, "Are the Greek Islands that big a deal to you, love?"

"Not really. It's just really nice to go there with you. No, the 'wow' was because I mean that much to you..."

Alex looked shocked. She cupped the little face in her hands and said in a slightly injured tone, "I love you more than life itself, don't you know that by now?"

Patty leaned into the hands. "Yes, I do. You have made that beautifully clear to me. Its just to know...well, that you feel the same way..." Tears poured from the eyes as she tried to express what she felt inside her heart.

"I know, my love, I know." Alex gently wiped away the tears and then brought the salty lips to hers and kissed Patty tenderly. It started out as a loving reassuring kiss, but something heated it up quickly. Suddenly Alex needed more; she deepened the kiss and found that Patty needed it, too. Soon Alex growled into the telephone for the driver to close all the windows and doors and get out.

When Vito arrived, the driver suggested he not stick his head in the car. "You might want to wait until they open a window for some air."

Vito smiled. "No problem, I'll wait. They deserve as much of that kind of activity as they can get."

About ten minutes later, Alex pulled back and looked at her watch. She opened up two windows for some air and said, "I wonder where Uncle Vito is? He's never late."

Through the now open window, two bright eyes smiled at them and Vito's voice said, "I was waiting for you to take a breath."

Alex and Patty looked at each other and then burst into a fit of giggles.

"Oops, sorry, Unc. Um, how long did you wait?"

"Ten minutes or so. It's okay. I really think you deserve it. Now, get going, you two. It's off to the Greek Islands for fun in the sun. Alexa, when you two come back, you will be strictly a civilian. Do you think you will be able to handle it?"

Alex looked at Patty snuggled up close. Resting her chin on top of Patty's head, she said softly, "With this one in my life, I know I will be just fine."

"How about a hug and kiss for your old uncle, girls, then off you go."

The girls pulled far enough apart so that first Alex and then Patty could hug and kiss the older man.

"Bye, Unc, I love you."

"I love you, too, my Alexa."

"I love you, too, Uncle Vito; and I'll miss you."

"I love you too, little one. I won't miss you though, because I'll have that hair ball you call a cat to keep me company."

The small woman laughed and then was pulled into the taller woman's embrace. They waved at the older man as the limo pulled away. Then he watched as the limo safely carried away the two most important people in his life for a well-deserved rest.

"Have fun you two," He called out as the limo left the drive way he walked to the house to get Fluffy and bring her to his place. "I know you will." He muttered to himself smiling.

The End

Printed in the United States
100144LV00002B/89/A